the Turnaway Girls

HAYLEY CHEWINS

CANDLEWICK PRESS

Copyright © 2018 by Hayley Chewins

First edition 2018

Library of Congress Catalog Card Number pending
ISBN 978-0-7636-9792-1

18 19 20 21 22 23 LSC 10 9 8 7 6 5 4 3 2 1

Printed in Crawfordsville, IN, U.S.A.

This book was typeset in Dante MT.

Candlewick Press
99 Dover Street
Somerville, Massachusetts 02144

visit us at www.candlewick.com

To all the girls who sing—or speak—
when they are told to be silent.

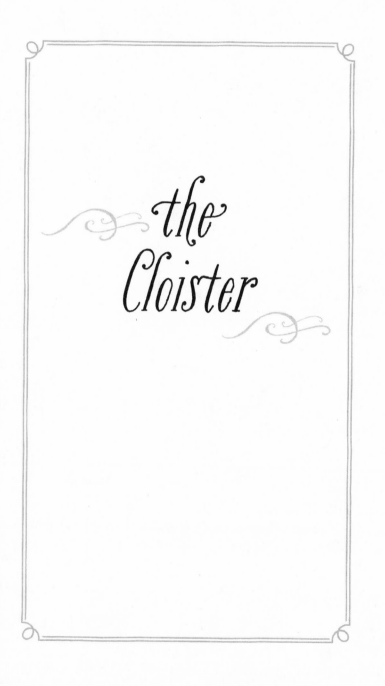

the
Cloister

Chapter One

Mother Nine says it's the wall that does it—fills the shimmer-room with music and gold. But I know it's someone on the other side.

I know it's a boy.

A boy who was born and wrapped in scrolls of music instead of blankets. A boy with bells crowning his head, the sea a chorus of thrash and spray behind him, lifting a stone-flute to his lip. Breathing songs into living.

Mother Nine says I couldn't tell a flickermoth's wing from a falling feather, but I know one thing: music needs a throat. Lungs and spit and gut's blood.

Don't tell, Delphernia. Don't.

I crouch, pressing my ear to damp stone. There's nothing there except the kind of silence only walls can make. It's a dead sort of quiet: a sound you'd expect to hear belowground and not above it. Even the sea hushes as though it's waiting for someone to make their penance.

I know it's not the wall that threads notes through the air like a crying bird—I know, I know, I know. Because when I push past the hard-kept silence of the lifeless wall, there are footsteps there, knuckle cracks. There's a tongue clicked and a cleared throat. I know he's there—I know. The sea rushes, howling, and splattered salt drips through starlit gaps.

I flinch, jumping back.

All my life I've been told that the sea surrounds the dome of the cloister just as the night sky holds the moon.

And that it swallows girls like me.

Don't tell.

The door to the shimmer-room opens like a cough, and the othergirls shuffle in. Their bare feet scuff the moss-spotted ground. They line up and I weave among them, moving past their stare-straight eyes to plant myself in the back, back row.

The hammering clangs of Mother Nine's foot-steps ring through my heels. The othergirls dip their chins. I gulp all my secrets down, but they churn in my stomach like a bad soup, clawing up my throat to get out.

Here she is—wrapped in muddied silks, cloister-wing feathers sewn to her sleeves to honor the First Mother. She makes a show of holy words, strikes a shard of hushingstone against the wall until it makes a *shhhh* sound and glows with fire.

Then she summons the music—from the boy, the boy outside, he's there, I know he's there—with one cold-uttered word: "Breathe."

Beyond the cloister, the city of Blightsend rings its bells.

And the boy behind the wall begins to play.

The othergirls lift their heads. Then Mother Nine says my name, and I know that it is time. Time for me to fail at kneading music into gold.

Making shimmer, Mother Nine calls it, because that's the thing with her sly-sticking tongue: she likes to turn words over until they mean nothing but what they aren't.

I walk until I'm close enough to feel the wall against my lips. Mother Nine holds up a mirror of polished gold and my face appears: dark eyes, brown skin. My hair's pulled back in a coiled bun, black curls fighting against being pinned. I pretend the bruise under my eye is only the shadow of a cloisterwing, picture it circling my head like a dark diadem.

I mutter the prayer we've been saying since we could speak: "Let me forget that I have eyes. Let me forget that I am an I."

"Go on," says Mother Nine, lowering the mirror.

I know what I'm supposed to do, not because I've ever actually done it but because I've watched the othergirls so many times—the ones in my class.

Maybe it's because I have a singing throat—*Don't tell, Delphernia, never tell*—or maybe it's because I am broken in my bones, but I can't make shimmer the way they do.

When they make shimmer, the othergirls face the wall with open palms, the music flowing through their bones. The notes gleam at their backs, thick-burnished threads, and they turn to face the strands of light, pulling music out of air, letting it sit heavily in their hands. They knead each piece until it becomes a knotted clump of gold. Mother Nine claps afterward—more of a warning than an applause—and we say another prayer to the First Mother: "Thank you for giving us the gift of knowing our place."

But there won't be any clapping now. Not for me. Because my hands are always empty. And empty hands, as Mother Nine likes to say, must be filled.

Filled with the hum of lashes.

Filled with blood.

Empty hands make for empty bellies — that's another thing she likes to say. And it's true. Because if we didn't make gold, the Custodian of Blightsend wouldn't drop seaflowers and hook-strung eels through the skydoor.

We'd starve, then.

Nothing grows in the cloister except lungmoss and half-dead tongue-fruit trees that don't even sprout petals. You can't eat darkness, and you can't chew stone. And you can't leave the cloister unless you're born in the right year. Unless you're led out by a bell-crowned boy to make gold for his pockets.

I show the wall the scars on my palms.

The thing is, I'm always too busy listening to the music to let it pass through me. When I was as small as an egg, I thought that I could be the same as the othergirls if only I tried hard enough. But even when I tried, my spine sprouted fingers. My knees became tight-fisted hands, my ankles knots. Every joint gripped every note that the stone-flutes sent rising, grabbed at every bright-quivering voice.

My bones take hold of the music now. It sticks, thickens my marrow like one of Mother Nine's stews. I wish the wall were mist so I could peer through and see him—see the boy with the stone-flute raised to his lip—I know he's there; I know. But I can't make mist out of stone. So I listen. I gather the music inside me. I lock it in, close myself up like an old chest of drawers. The musician wavers, unsure if he should continue. He can sense that I'm not making shimmer. That there's something wrong. That *I* am wrong.

I want to twist my mouth into a mocking, ask Mother Nine if rock ever hesitates, but before I can, she untucks a twiggy switch from the folds of her skirt and slices the back of my hand with it. A stripe of redness appears, raising the skin across my finger bones.

The music stops, and a truth settles in my belly like a bird folding its wings into a nest. I will never see the sky in its entirety. The sky wouldn't ever want to set its eyes on me.

Mother Nine says, "The whisper-room—now,"

and I know I will not hear the rest of the songs. The songs the othergirls turn into gold.

The songs that no girl in Blightsend is ever allowed to echo.

The door to the shimmer-room closes behind me. The passageway of black stone is unlit, but I know the way well to the whisper-room.

I press the little music I heard into the curve of my ribs. I want to keep it for later—for my time in the hollow tree. My feet tap against stone, but I take care not to make any rhythm.

I might lock songs in my bones for safekeeping, but that doesn't mean they belong to me.

I'm a turnaway girl and so I know: music belongs to the Masters.

Chapter Two

I do not look at the hollow tree on my way to the whisper-room. I can smell the damp of its ungrowing branches, but I do not look. If I glimpse one leaf, I will run to it, climb inside. I will fill it with singing.

And singing's something I do only after bedtime, when I can be alone with wings. With the cloisterwings. My cloisterwings.

It's safe then. Mother Nine makes a noise of dreams and her cheeks are marked with pillow creases and I know she won't wake up. She takes foul-smelling droplets to her tongue each night, and not even a stone-rattling storm can wake her. Not even a girl blowing on her eyelids.

Don't tell.

I walk down Teeth Row, the cobbled lane that keeps the trees on one side and our rooms on the other. I pass eating-rooms, sleeping-rooms, scrub-bing-rooms, the shimmer-room far behind me. But I can't think of eating or sleeping. I can't even think of a hot bath. The ache in my hand is dulling now, and I've lost all thoughts of switches and bruises—but I'm thinking of another pain.

Pain no bruise could show.

The whisper-room's door is as heavy as the one that closes the music inside the shimmer-room. The air is just as cold. But while the shimmer-room is made of stone and more stone—gloom and more gloom—the whisper-room has faces in it. They're chiseled into the walls in an army of stillnesses, lanterns of hushingstone arranged to light their eyes.

It's beautiful, the whisper-room is, beautiful and fright-filled. Because they're not just any faces, the ones that adorn the walls. They're the faces of the Mothers.

And their eyes know exactly how awful I have been.

The First Mother is there, a cloisterwing sitting in her open palm. I have been sent here to tell her I'm sorry. To tell the cloisterwing, too.

I don't mind the thought of praying to a bird. I

sing to them every night, all my secrets held in the timbre of my voice. But even the First Mother—dead as she is—knows I would sooner give her my right ear than a paean dug from the mud of my heart.

Still, I bend my neck and touch my fingers to my lips when I see her gold-dusted brow. She was the first turnaway girl in Blightsend. The best. The quietest. They say she floated instead of walking, her soundless feet a tribute to the silence girls must leave upon our land.

Mother Nine's heels leave no such silence, but if I questioned her, she'd say the rules are for me and not for Mothers. She'd say she is the rule—and I the one to obey it.

She would be right.

I kneel. I count my breaths.

"I forgot," I whisper. "I forgot to let the music flow through. I'm—"

I can't say it.

All I wanted—all I've ever wanted—was to keep something beautiful for myself. I shouldn't have to make penance for that. Not when I live in the cloister, in a dome of hushingstone that keeps everything out—everything—including the sky and sea.

The carved eyes of the Mothers peel me open like a slit tongue-fruit. I'm supposed to keep my gaze lowered out of respect, but still—I look up. I look into the First Mother's eyes.

I want to prove that she can't hurt me. That even if she was the best turnaway girl in Blightsend, she's gone now. Gone and dead—like the seven Mothers after her. Which means I'm better than she is in at least one way: I am alive.

She looks at me with a quizzing smile.

And then I break another rule. I stand and walk toward her portrait until I'm close enough to lick it.

I half expect the ceiling to crumble. Half expect the First Mother to slap me, add to the artful bruises Mother Nine's left behind. But the walls remain unmoving. Everything is still.

I trace the cloisterwing's shape with my finger.

In Histories, we learned that the First Mother carved the cloisterwings out of Blightsend's hushingstone—carefully, as all things hushingstone should be handled, with a sculptor's knife. I know my cloisterwings—the ones I sing to each night—come to the world hatched from speck-and-fleck eggs, but I like to think of the tale as truth. I like to think that stone as cold as this can make something flying—something as glossy and proud as a bird with out-stretched wings.

Rushing steps echo across cobbles, louder and louder, and my fingertip catches against the cloisterwing's pointed beak. I run back to the center of the room. I kneel again. I dip my pounding head.

The door opens.

Mother Nine breathes ragged breaths, walking a circle about me. "Do you know, Delphernia, why I never look you in the eye?"

I stare at the ground. "You don't look at a thing invisible," I say. "You don't look at a thing that is not to be seen."

"And what of you?" She slaps the twig-switch against her palm.

My skin is a sack, and I'm wriggling inside it.

"Turnaway girls are not seen—they see. Turnaway girls are not heard—they hear."

"Good," she says. "I was starting to think you'd forgotten everything I'd ever taught you." She holds out a pale, unblemished hand. She was a good turnaway girl. She's not broken in her bones. She doesn't need to be put back together with whispers and slaps and penance.

I grip her fingers, get to my feet.

She curls her silks around me. The feathers on her sleeves quiver. I want to rip them off her. She doesn't deserve them. She hates cloisterwings. Hates anything that sings.

"I've told you before, Delphernia—you've decided who you are instead of letting me tell you. That's why you can't make shimmer." She shifts, one hand gripping my shoulder. Her scattered glancing lands on me for a second—only a second.

"Yes, Mother Nine," I say.

"And what is the one thing you must always remember?"

I wait as long as I can before I say the words. Because even though I know they're true, my body doesn't want to say them. My jaw aches.

"Girls with singing throats are swallowed by the sea."

"Swallowed by the sea," Mother Nine repeats.

"Swallowed by the sea," I whisper.

Mother Nine has always punished me, but this

week has been worse than ever. I suppose it's because the Festival of Bells is nearing, and soon the Custodian will be here, watching us. Watching her. And I am a blot that won't rub out. I am the only turnaway girl in Blightsend's history who can't make gold out of melodies.

"You know I only want the best for you," she says.

I nod, even though I don't, I don't, I don't. You can't want the best for someone and wish for them to bleed.

"It's the truth," she says. "About girls with singing throats. The sea has made many dinners of them." She flicks her chin at the door, and I move toward it.

She follows close behind. Then she bends to touch her lips to my ear. "Remember that and you'll keep your lungs from tasting salt."

Chapter Three

It's past midnight before I'm able to uncoil from under my bedclothes, spread my arms out in the wet-smelling dark. Bare feet. Bare heart.

I feel Mother Nine following me as I tiptoe across Teeth Row, even though I know she's snug under heavy quilts in her sleeping-room. I hear her heels banging against stone, her switch scraping a trail along the ground. I turn, sharp-shouldered, but there's no one there. Of course there's no one there.

I sprint the rest of the way across the Row. The cold wrings my bones in its hands, but the thought of the softness of lungmoss I'll feel beneath my feet when I get to the trees, the trees, the trees, makes it worth the ache. Here I am: skimming the damp, the crooked ghosts of branches gathering me close. I love all the trees in the cloister, but the hollow tree is my favorite.

The cloisterwings sigh among half-dead leaves, waiting for me to sing to them.

I loosen a dangling strip of the hollow tree's bark and press it to my tongue. It tastes of the rain that pours through the skydoor once every week when Mother Nine opens it to receive our food from the Custodian and our water from the clouds, when the cloisterwings are locked in bent-gold cages so that they can't escape. It tastes of how it must feel to see the whole sky in one go. It tastes of having wings.

I grab one of the drooping branches and hoist myself into the hollow tree's belly, sliding down, down, down. My finger bones prickle as I settle into the joy of the dark. In the dark, I am hidden. In the dark, I can sing. In the dark, I am as much cloisterwing as girl.

I close my eyes. And then all I know is the sound of the sea and the gap-whistling wind and the cloisterwings' rustling feathers. My voice stitches their melodies together.

I draw the music from my side—the music I stowed there hours before—into my throat. I yawn my mouth open.

The night-pocket fills with my voice.

Sea-waves beat and beat. I can hear the cloister-wings tapping their beaks, the twitch of feathers and the crick-crack of claws. They lift out of their nests and shift their wings in the branches around me, cutting a glide through air.

Then a quick wing brushes my bruised cheek, and my eyes open to a glaring shot of light, a twisting spiral above my head. I squint, unaccustomed to anything other than the thickness of the dark, and make out a cloisterwing flapping its wings up and up, out of the hollow tree's trunk. For a moment I think Mother Nine's come with her hushingstone lantern to singe my skin off.

Then I realize: I've made light-strands. The way the othergirls do in the shimmer-room—but out of my own singing. The strands move slowly as poured sap, tangling and untangling, looping and unlooping. I stretch my arm up, touch one with the tip of a finger, and it loosens from the air and settles in my palm, curled up like a sleeper.

I've made this.

I've pushed my own voice through marrow.

The cloisterwings must have wanted me to know. They must have wanted me to open my eyes. To see it. This.

My fingers are pulsing with stick-of-pin tingles, and the slice on the back of my hand itches and stings as if my skin's speaking its own language, but eventually I'm able to knead the light-strand into gold. At least—I think it's gold. But as I cup it like a warm egg, something crimps in my hands like a heartbeat.

Pa-pum.

A flickermoth must be buzzing its wings at my skin.

It happens again—three sets of couplet beats this time.

Pa-pum, pa-pum, pa-pum.

That's no flickermoth.

I open my hands, and there, sitting all folded up, is a small golden bird.

It lifts off my palm to drift on air-tides as if it were made for flying. As if I made it for flying.

Because that's what I did.

Instead of making a dead clump of gold—gold for a door handle, an earring, a spoon—I have sung a bird with a beating heart.

I can't make shimmer—but I can make something living. Now the living thing dives overhead.

"Hello, little bird," I say. "Where did you come from?" I hold out my finger, and the bird lands there, tilts its head. "Don't worry," I whisper. "I'll look after you."

I'm about to fold it in my hands again when it flies straight up through the light-strands I haven't yet kneaded, out of the hollow tree.

"Wait!" I cry, gripping the inside of the tree trunk with my fingernails, pulling myself up and out.

I land in the wet and slip and fall, my sliced hand smacked between my chest and the ground. Pain crackles like snapping twigs beneath my skin. I scramble to my feet.

The golden bird floats in a dipping line along the cloister's outer wall, spinning ribbons of light against stone.

"Don't go," I call. "Don't—"

When I reach the bird, its wings are brushing the wall as though it wants to escape. I hold my hand out, but it hurries away, as if it's following a sound or a smell. For a moment, I hear it. A stone-flute. Even though nothing I've ever learned in Histories says that a Master would be out here this late at night.

I press my cheek against the wall and wait. And wait. And wait. Wait for the sound to come back. I forget about the bird as it flits above my head. I forget about my bruises, too—forget all the bruises I've ever had.

When the Master begins to play again, melodies gather on the end of my tongue. I can't stop them—they drop off, note by note, and I am singing. I keep my eyes open this time, waiting for the strands of light to run right through me. Within moments, they are mellowing at my back, blowing around me like a skirt. I take one in my hands and knead it. There it is again: *pa-pum, pa-pum.* Another bird escapes through my fingers. My bones feel lit from the inside.

Strand after strand, the light knits in my palms. My voice sets the night ablaze, the wings of more and more golden birds shivering into being until they're brushing against my knuckles, eyelashes, earlobes, shaking moonlight from delicate feathers. Until I am surrounded by them.

Then they disperse and gather again, flying from me in a cloud of whispered chirrups. They push through a gap in the cloister's outer wall.

"But how?" I breathe.

I stagger in their direction, reach for them, reach for the birds I sang into living, but the last one escapes before I can get to it.

The cloisterwings, twirling through the branches above my head, twitch as though they're flying and sleeping at the same time, ruffling their feathers and snapping their beaks, cawing at a sky they'll never swoop against.

I press my eye to the slit, blinking against stone. Gold wings float over the sea. Float away from me.

And then the stone-flute falls silent.

And I hear the sound of someone swallowing. All at once it's as though I'm looking into a mirror and not through a wall, not at the sea, not at the wings of birds that I have made and lost.

Because on the other side of the wall is an eye, sunken against brown skin. Wide and looking at the world as if it hurts to see it, to see anything at all. Dark as dark will ever be.

It looks like my eye, but it can only be the eye of the stone-flautist. The eye of the boy who made music on the other side of the wall, the sea sucking at his back as I've always imagined. A Master.

My eye stays open, frozen against the gap, while the boy's eye blinks. *Pa-pum.* This time it's my own heart. *Pa-pum, pa-pum, pa-pum.*

And that beating pulls me back into the world I know.

I press off the wall.

I turn and run, trampling soil and lungmoss, ducking under low-hanging branches, until I am standing on Teeth Row again, my breath wound up like thread on a spool within me.

My tongue is a piece of bitter fish in my mouth.

I sprint again, back to the sleeping-room. I huddle under salt-clean quilts, nursing all my sore places — my swollen cheek, my burning heart — and it's only once the black soil and bits of lungmoss have dried on my toes that I'm taken by sleep, dragged through dreams about sliced-off fingers, walls with eyes, and sad, unflying birds.

Chapter Four

Usually I don't like Histories, but today's lesson might as well have wings. Because today we are learning about the Sea-Singer—as a warning and a warning only.

One thing Mother Nine has told me about the Sea-Singer is that the hollow tree's death was all her fault. That she was the one who started the fire in the cloister when she was my age. (Easy enough to do, in a place made of hushingstone, which blares into flame if struck at any suitable angle.)

Mother Nine wants me to hate the Sea-Singer and her singing and the way she went to the waves for it. Mother Nine raised her and she says she was always trouble, trouble, trouble. But I can't think of the Sea-Singer as a strife-maker. Her fire made a space for me to sing.

And the truth is, I dream of fires.

Of burning the cloister down.

Don't tell.

Don't tell.

Don't tell.

Mother Nine's staring is like a graze.

"I knew her best," she says.

She means she's counted the Sea-Singer's faults as keenly as she's counted mine. Which is part of the reason I love the Sea-Singer, even if she's dead and gone like the First Mother. She must have known what it was like to wear Mother Nine's words, always, like a wet-clinging dress.

Mother Nine lets us stand in a scatter on Teeth Row, tells us to look up. We've always seen the Sea-Singer — since cribhood we've been seeing her there, carved into the cloister's high, smooth dome, the sky-door over her heart. Waves crash around her. She's wearing the sea as a dress. Accents of gold brush her cheeks and brow, and stings of light twinkle through tiny holes in the stone around her head, so that she's crowned by the sun itself. In my dreams, she hums lullabies against my hurtless cheeks. *Don't be silent,* she says. *Sing.*

But Mother Nine carved her there with her own hands to remind us that girls with singing throats are swallowed by the sea.

No matter. My heart can do its own reading.

I shake my head, trying to rid my mind of thoughts—thoughts about singing in the hollow tree, about those spark-birds skimming moon-trailed waves. Thoughts about the eye I saw on the other side of the wall and the boy it belonged to—the Master who saw me. The Master who heard me.

"Of the Sea-Singer," says Mother Nine, "I will tell you three things." Her tongue clenches around the syllables. She clears her throat, and it sounds like she's clearing her chest of dust.

Three things in twelve years. Mother Nine is stingy with her secrets.

"The first is that she was born of a good family— let them not be blamed."

She dips her chin, touches fingers to lips—a bless- ing for the Sea-Singer's kin—and so do the othergirls. I stare at their faces, turned cheek after turned cheek.

I've known them all my life—since we were brought here, placed in lungmossy cribs—but I've never spoken to any of them for more than a few minutes. When we do speak, it's to point out things we already know. They don't have thoughts of their own, the othergirls. I've learned to speak to trees—and to birds—instead.

"The second," says Mother Nine, "is this. The Sea-Singer was the Ninth King's turnaway girl—before she became his wife and queen. She reigned well until she conspired to sing a song at Sorrowhall twelve years ago. A song of her own making. She desecrated the Garden of All Silences in front of Blightsend's Masters, and the sea punished her that very night. A storm rose—the worst in our island's history—to snatch her from her bed. Ever since, the beds in the palace have been arranged so that the sleeper always faces the sea. Even dreamers must be watchful."

I force my lips into a dry pucker to stop my smile—eyes watering, ears ringing. The fire-setter sang in the Ninth King's own home. I am not supposed to be impressed, of course. I am supposed to be appalled. Or, at least, uninterested, as the othergirls are.

"And the third," says Mother Nine.

I want her not to say the third. Not yet. I want to wait. I don't want it to be over. I imagine the words delivered to me on the wings of a bird—not a golden bird. *Don't think it, Delphernia. Don't tell.*

Mother Nine is careful to make her words deliberate and slow. But underneath them I can hear the growl of hating. "Let it be known that the Sea-Singer, devoured by waves for her disobedience, so shamed the royal family that the Ninth King grew ill with a case of crinkle-lung and died a terrible, unbreathing death. In the Sea-Singer's palm rests his last day."

Mother Nine pauses. She swallows as if she's got a lump of hardened tree sap stuck in her throat.

"Thank the First Mother that treachery doesn't run in the blood. The Sea-Singer came from a good family, and from her came the Childer-Queen—a strong ruler who knows that Blightsend's laws are made to be kept."

A queen. A Childer-Queen. That's the first I've heard of her.

I look up at the Sea-Singer. You'd think her face would be a slant of horror, but there's something else in her eyes. I know it and I have always known it: she was glad to die for singing. She knew that the sea would take her if she sang. She made a sound anyway. My heart fills with the rustling of feathers.

I'm so busy staring up at her face—staring and staring and definitely not thinking about walls and stone-flutes and dark-eyed Masters—that I can't stop the question from escaping my lips: "Why did Mother Nine carve your eyes with fighting in them?"

And then the othergirls have scattered and I know Mother Nine has heard.

She grabs my right hand—hard. I yelp and try to wrench away, but she only grips my already hurt fingers tighter. She pulls a twisted wooden clamp, bent like a bird's broken beak, from the folds of her skirt.

She tears the nail from my thumb with it.

I heave, falling to my knees. It's not only my hand that's in pain—it's my whole body, from the roots of my curls to my clenched toes, all burning, burning, burning.

This has never happened before. Mother Nine has bruised me for opening my mouth, she's made me bleed for not making shimmer, but she's never torn a part of me away.

I want to ask her why she did it, but I already know the answer. The question itself holds its reply, like the yolk inside a boiled cloisterwing egg.

She did it because she hates the Sea-Singer.

She did it because she hates me.

Chapter Five

I'm glad when Mother Nine chooses the babies' sleeping-room as my scolding place — you can't use switches there.

The little ones are silent in their lungmossy cribs until one of them opens her mouth, makes a sound that could split a ceiling — even the ceiling of hushing-stone that looms over our heads. Mother Nine picks her up, swaying her back and forth to soothe her. "In there," she says, nodding toward a chest, scuffed and stained after years of salted damp. "Bandages."

My hands quake as I search for a strip of cloth to stop the bleeding.

Mother Nine only speaks again once I've wound the flickermoth silk around my thumb. "Do you know what our rules are for, Delphernia?"

My eyes are bleary with tears and I don't care, I don't care, I don't care what they're for. The bawling baby seems to feel the same way.

The room is full of babies, but this one is the newest. Every girl who's born in Blightsend is given a mirror on the day of her birth. And what she does with it determines whether she ends up here or out in the world, scrubbing the floors the Masters tread their shoes on.

This baby was dropped off last week, wrapped in an embroidered cloak. She must have turned away from her reflection, like the rest of us did. That's why they call us turnaway girls. Because we turned our faces from polished gold instead of scouring it for our own eyes.

Girls who make shimmer need to be selfless, need to hold whole worlds in their bones, need to listen, listen, listen. They need to turn away from who they are and who they wish to be.

"The rules," says Mother Nine, "are there to teach you how to survive. You want to live, don't you?"

"Yes," I say.

But that's only partly true.

Because what I do not say is this: I want to live outside.

"Right," says Mother Nine. "Here's an education for your eyes."

She marches to the back of the room, where she places the baby, spine bent with screaming, on a table engraved with crashing waves.

"What are you going to do?" I say. A hurting's coming, I'm sure of it. My thumb beats in an aching counterpoint to my heart.

"After the Sea-Singer was swallowed by the sea," says Mother Nine, circling a thumb and index finger around each of the baby's white wrists, "the Ninth King passed a law. It requires that part of every turn-away girl's heart be removed."

"Removed?" I am clutching my own wrist now.

A hurting's coming, a hurting's coming—

Mother Nine goes on holding the baby's wrists. She stands very still, closes her metallic eyes, dips her chin, her palms facing the child.

And then I see what she's doing.

Sometimes I forget that Mother Nine used to be a girl like me.

The baby's sobs are coming out hoarse like a soughing wind.

And Mother Nine is letting them drift through her bones.

She's making shimmer.

But the strands at her back are not lustrous gold—they're crooked bands of silver and shadow. They jerk in the air like birds with broken wings.

She turns toward the grime-gleaming strands, takes them in her hands and kneads them. I stand on my tiptoes to see what she's doing—what she's *making*.

When her fingers unfurl, I see it—a small brace-let of dull silver.

She puts it around the baby's wrist, leaves it there for a few breaths, and the little thing falls silent—her lips a neat line, her blue eyes dripping blank-blinking tears. Mother Nine takes the bracelet off again and pockets it. There's a faint darkness where the metal used to be, as though storming clouds have mistaken the baby's skin for the sky.

A bead of bitterness collects behind my tongue. "You took out the part of her that cries."

Mother Nine undresses the baby and crumples up her sleeping-robe, fetching a mud-dyed smock for her instead.

"You took out the part of her that cries," I say again.

"I've rid her of questions," Mother Nine says, holding the baby up. "She's satisfied now. She's content."

I look around the room. All the other babies are sleeping peacefully, as though sleep itself is dreaming of them.

And I know that she's taken their questions, too.

I run along the rows of cribs.

Every single one has a ring of cloudy grayness sweeping her skin.

"You've done it to all of them," I say. My voice is a fist.

I've never seen a scar on my arm, but maybe I wasn't looking hard enough. I didn't even know I needed to look. I start to roll up my sleeves.

Then Mother Nine is kneeling before me, smoothing my cuffs. "You don't have one," she says.

I stare at the wrinkled space between her eyebrows. "I don't?"

"The day the Sea-Singer's death was announced," she says, looking past me, "was the day you arrived at the cloister. There was a festival in Blightsend to celebrate the new law—the Festival of Questions. There was music while I did it. Your class was the first. I bundled you into your crib—you always slept so deeply, as though you had lullabies swirling your veins—and, as the others began to cry, I drew it out of them. All their wanting and all their needing. I made warped silver of their longings. I bound them with it. I showed them how useless it was—just dead metal to them and nothing warm, nothing that would ever make anything better. And they stopped. One by one, they stopped. No tantrums since."

"I don't understand. Did you remove their ability to cry? Or their ability to ask?"

"A cry and a question come from the same place in a girl's heart."

"And me—"

"I couldn't. I couldn't."

Mother Nine said the baby was satisfied. Content. But I am not. I have questions like claw tips in my stomach. I have a buzzing in my blood that never stops. A buzzing I can't portion into words now. I swallow and swallow, but my tongue stays fat, filling my mouth like a spoonful of seaflower stew.

"Do you know who the Sea-Singer was, Delphernia?" Mother Nine is whispering. Her eyes are brimming with unfalling tears. "She was a girl who asked questions. She became a woman who asked questions. And there is nothing Blightsend hates more than that."

She gets to her feet. She runs a hand over the top of my head.

"I gave you a gift, Delphernia. I left your heart alone. For the First Mother's sake, don't waste all that by drenching your own lungs."

Gift. A soft kiss of a word. Mother Nine could never give a gift. What she gave me was a burden, heavy as a spadeful of soil. What she gave me was a way of knowing what I lack. If I didn't have questions, I'd be like the othergirls. I'd be good at making shimmer and I'd be chosen by one of the Masters and I'd never know that I was missing singing.

"Go on, now," Mother Nine mutters. "Be a good girl."

The thing is, though, good girls don't sing in

hollow trees, don't meet eyes with Masters on the wrong side of walls. They don't lift their gaze in the whisper-room, don't walk toward the First Mother's face. They don't smile when they hear of the Sea-Singer's transgressions, the fires she lit in caught gardens, the way she desecrated the Garden of All Silences by flinging her voice against metal.

But I do.

That's how I know I'll never be good—unless I cut out my own heart entirely.

Unless Mother Nine plucks my voice right out of my throat.

Chapter Six

We lie on our backs on the cobbles of Teeth Row—
me and the othergirls. The mist loosens curls from
my pinned bun, ties white knots around my ankles. I
can barely see the Sea-Singer's eyes through the haze.
But I squint, staring into them.

Mother Nine says the staring's for our own
good—to remember who we are not to become.
Which doesn't explain why she made the Sea-Singer's
eyes so full of I-am-right. But I won't ask again. I only
have so many fingernails.

"This will be your final Silence lesson before the
Festival of Bells," says Mother Nine. "You'd be wise to
practice well." She glances in my direction. And then
she motions with her hands to call the cloisterwings.

Everyone works here, even the birds, and the cloisterwings know that Mother Nine's flicked fingers mean food. They're clever creatures, they really are. They know a thing or two about pleasing.

The cloisterwings swoop from trees, black-shining wings beating through air, cawing a rippling, layered song.

We can't make shimmer—or anything else— from the songs of birds, but they help us to practice our Silence: stilling our thoughts until they center only on the forever-ribbons of the notes.

The cloisterwings don't make songs that start in one place and end in another. Their songs travel in circles, always coming back to the beginning. The First Mother taught them to sing like that. She taught them circle-songs because she believed that where we begin is where we end.

The othergirls smart as the birds dive and swivel, whipping up air and wearing smooth trails of mist as cloaks. They're scared of the cloisterwings because the legend goes that they were born of stone, which makes their wings as sharp as knives.

It's true that they have hard edges—the tips of their feathers could slice tongue-fruit skins. And it

suits me that the othergirls find them frightening—
the trees are all my own that way.

But I've been up close to the cloisterwings when
they're tucked in their nests. In the night, in the quiet,
I have touched their ball-of-thread heads. I have sung
to them, reminded them of soaring, and seen them
flying in gentle circles above me.

I know what the othergirls don't.

I know that it's only when we're all awake and
there's a chance of them being caught by Mother
Nine—plucked for feathers or smacked for singing
too loudly—that they spin in rapid whirls. When
they don't feel threatened, they are not a threat. You
could hold them in one hand if you weren't as small-
handed as I am.

I close my eyes when I hear Mother Nine's hammering heels. I don't want to see her, but I can't stop
listening to her steps. I can't stop following rhythms. I
tap a finger on the ground and a pattern of low notes
rumbles in my throat. I press my tongue to the roof
of my mouth to stop it. The othergirls breathe slow
and slower.

I exhale.

No one noticed.

The cloisterwings draw out wing-beaten rhythms, chirping out looping trills, and it's only then that I remember: I'm supposed to let their singing rush through me. But I'm not easy to open. The closed drawers in my knees and knuckles stick from damp. My blood is thick as cobble-mud.

The birds' music — and wind, wing-wallop — fills the cloister to bursting. It fills me up, too. I clench my teeth to keep from singing. I try to remember that the blood's barely dried on my torn thumb.

Here they are — the instruments of my closed world. Mother Nine's *click, click, click*ing on uneven cobbles. The othergirls' breathing, harmonious as flutes. The thrashing call of the sea and the lifting chords of the cloisterwings' choir. The slice-soar of their wings through a thick breath of mist.

There's a grumble in my throat again. A single note. It climbs up from the base of my spine. My lips part.

And I swallow it down.

Because Mother Nine's face is over mine, its folds a shadowed dance of threats. I tangle my fingers together, all bandages and scabs, and dig them against my stomach. I try to make myself as small as a dropped feather.

"Lungmoss will speak my name long before a Master chooses a girl like you."

I look past her snarl. Through stirring wings, I can see the Sea-Singer's eyes. Unblinking. Unwavering.

Mother Nine steps away from me and scatters bits of dried seaflower across the ground.

The cloisterwings fall silent, dropping from flight to peck at stale morsels.

Chapter Seven

Today is the day—the Festival of Bells. Everything ringing into change. Or silenced for the rest of time. Either I'll be chosen, or I'll be stuck. As good as dead. Kept from the sky until I'm only bones.

I drag my nails over the scabs on my knuckles, pretend it's Mother Nine's skin I'm scratching. I'm tangled in a net she knitted. I try not to think of my future: Mother Nine growing older, running the questions and cries of little girls through her bones. Me, picking her teeth. Folding her silks into drawers. A prisoner. A turnaway girl who cannot make shimmer. Forever.

I pretend at preparations, slicking my skin with wet loam and sap, wishing I could rinse this past week out of my heart. I'm supposed to be using salt, too, to scrub away rough patches on my elbows and knees, but I have too many cuts and bruises to do that—too many scratches that would turn to blood-flowers. I lower myself into a stone tub of hot seawater. My hand stings like a fistful of pins.

Then it's time for the dresses.

We—me and the othergirls in my year—scuttle through dim passages, past rooms of backlit curls, lips that might as well be stitched. Rooms and rooms and rooms of younger girls with quiet, unquestioning hearts. And to think I used to wonder how Mother Nine managed us all.

We file into our sleeping-room. I expect to find dresses laid out on beds, but there are none. A draft slinks past like a sneering laugh, but the othergirls don't seem worried. They do what they do best: wait for Mother Nine to arrive. They might as well be sleep-standing. They might as well be made of stone.

Then Mother Nine appears in the doorway, her eyes red. The veins in her neck bulge like hungry slugs. "There's something that needs to be done first," she says. "Can't risk the stains." That's when I see the needle. "Your left ears need to be pierced. To set you apart from the soapstresses."

But that can't be true—not entirely. Anyone

could tell a turnaway girl from a soapstress. I'm sure they have their own breed of sufferings, but they're not taught to empty their bones for the sounds of cloisterwings and the songs of walls. Their questions have not been cut out like a troublesome lung.

No—this is something different. A way of reminding us that we are more ear than tongue.

Mother Nine lines us up. When she gets to me, she takes my head in her hands, pushing against my bruised cheek. Then she slides the needle through the lobe of my ear, stops the hole with a dangling hook of gold.

I close my eyes, and when I open them, I see blood. I wonder how much I've lost this week—and how much I've got left. The floor grows blotches.

Mother Nine fetches the dresses, piles of fabric in her thin-wrinkled arms.

I watch the othergirls slip into dirt-dyed silk, storm-cloud scars marking their wrists. Then I pull the stiff fabric over my head. The dress hangs around my body like a curtain. The shoes are a different tale, though: gold-stitched silk slippers with wooden heels. I hold one up to a lit hushingstone shard, watching embroidered patterns shimmer like a hidden language of leaf and wave and moon. I squish my feet into them and pretend I'm walking high above hurts, skimming my toes on a gilded pool of music.

We are arranged in kneeling lines on the cobbles of Teeth Row — all the turnaway girls in my year. We're packed arm to arm, the most talented at the front. I want to grab someone's wrist and scream — scream for us all to be let out. But I don't. I can't. No one would listen to a turnaway girl, anyway.

The closed skydoor is battered by the wind, its stone hinges grinding like a pestle and mortar. I try not to look up.

"Sea-Singer," I whisper, "hear me. Please. Please. Give me a miracle. Let one of them choose me."

Then I hear it: a knock from above, as though heaven has arrived to take a bowl of soup. Mother Nine drags the limp-legged ladder over to the sky-door. She climbs it, step by step, its rungs creaking beneath her weight. She turns keys in their stuck locks.

The door to the Sea-Singer's heart smacks open and Mother Nine hooks it into place. Then she climbs down and waits. The ladder shivers.

And then I see: gold slippers on worn wood. White ankles. The hem of a coat, edged with glinting stitches. The back is embroidered with closed mouths.

The man belonging to the coat steps noiselessly onto cobbles, turns to face us. His eyes are surrounded by moons of color, as if he's never slept a night in all of Histories. I can see him clearly, but I can't hear him. He wears no bells. If silence had a face, it would have his face. He's as silent as we are taught to be.

"Girls," says Mother Nine, "this is Mr. Crowwith, the Custodian of Blightsend. He's come to introduce the best Masters of our city."

She touches her fingers to her lips and closes her eyes. We all do the same. Even I obey. This man could decide my path.

"Turnaway girls," says Mr. Crowwith, walking to stand before us. His feet glide rather than click. His voice is low and rhythmless. "For the first eighty-nine years of Blightsend's rich history, your kind did not leave the cloister—ever. You made shimmer for the island, sent up into the hands of Masters as the King saw fit."

A fire flickers in my gut, but the othergirls only nod in agreement.

"It was the Third King, Lull Harpermall, who said that rewards should go to those who reward our ears," continues Mr. Crowwith. "The tradition he founded has blossomed into one of the most hallowed on our rocky shores. Every twelve years, we celebrate a Festival of Bells, and the seventeen best Masters in Blightsend—all born in the year of the previous Festival—are chosen. On this day, each of these best Masters chooses a turnaway girl born the same year to make gold for his pockets. This year, the Childer-Queen has personally sewn the best Masters' cuffs and hems with golden bells engraved with her name. And now they will make their pick of you."

He steps to the side and claps. His fingers are slender and delicate, but the sound is like the clattering of a dropped bowl.

It doesn't bother me, though. Because the clapping means they're coming.

The Masters.

The best Masters.

My beginning—or my end.

Chapter Eight

Mother Nine has taught us what Masters wear, but seeing it is a different kettle of eel.

The first Master I've ever glimpsed toe to nose climbs down the ladder with slow steps. He is dressed in music.

His entire suit—a collarless jacket with wide sleeves that skims his knees, a fitted shirt and stiff trousers—is covered in gold bells. The edge of his headdress is fringed with them, too. And, because he's one of the best Masters, his cuffs and hems are sewn with chiming clinks. His silken wood-heeled boots swirl with embroidered color: with the shapes of waves and vines. He looks as though he grew straight from the ground like that—all pride and shine. He looks as though he hasn't ever heard the word *never*. As if it doesn't exist in his bright language.

The bells sound like falling mist as he walks.

The othergirls do not move. Their eyes are fixed like stone saucers.

"Turnaway girls," Mr. Crowwith says, "this is Pall Wavethrone. The first of Blightsend's best Masters for this Festival of Bells."

He motions to the boy, who unclips the instrument sheathed at his hip and holds it to his mouth. Then Mr. Crowwith chooses an othergirl from the front row with an impatient flick of his fingers. The girl stands beside the Master and turns rippling notes into beams of light as he plays, handing a smooth tangle of gold to him when she's finished. He dips his chin to avoid her eyes and takes the gift.

My eyes itch with wanting to look at the hollow tree, but I keep them on my own hands.

Don't tell, Delphernia.

Mr. Crowwith walks to meet Mother Nine's ear. Mother Nine nods, and the othergirl follows the Master up the ladder and out the skydoor. I imagine her seeing the whole sky for the first time. I bite my tongue.

I watch the door, expecting the next Master to be the same as the first. But right away, I know this Master is different.

This Master is wearing a dress.

Her shoes are wood-heeled, silk, stitched with gold, like Pall Wavethrone's. But a belled hem dances at her bare calves. Her dress is the deep red of soapstress silk, sewn with so many golden bells that only specks of the color peek through. Every step she takes is steady, as though each one is a word and she's saying *I belong here* with every three she takes. There's something about her that makes me think she could tiptoe across the sea. She looks made of light, all slants. She looks set for flying.

My lungs buzz.

She is what I dream of being.

A girl-Master.

Mother Nine's always said only boys can be Masters, but my eyes are proving her wrong. A girl-Master stands before me. Before all of us.

She's wearing the traditional headdress, and beneath it strands of white-wisp hair play at her pinkish cheeks. She looks like a princess and a Master and a rebel. She looks like she could crack the stone dome of the cloister with one breathed note. Her palms are golden.

She practically skips toward Mr. Crowwith, who

seems to both recognize her and not recognize her. He frowns, brushing at his graying hair. All the furrows in his face seem to grow deeper, as though they've been inked. I hold my breath, waiting to see what will happen. Waiting to hear her name.

"Turnaway girls," says Mr. Crowwith, "this is—"

"My name," says the girl-Master, "is Linna. Linna Lundd."

Mr. Crowwith whispers viciously in her ear, the words blurred.

Mother Nine stares at the ground and the othergirls follow suit, but I have to watch.

This girl makes the roots of my eyelashes prickle.

Mr. Crowwith has taken hold of her arm and he's still speaking in her ear when she tugs away from him, unsheathes her stone-flute.

And plays the most wing-full song I have ever heard.

It sounds like a tree growing. It sounds like a kiss from a mother you never knew. It sounds like the color of the sky in the morning, before anyone else is awake.

An othergirl steps forward, lets the notes run through her. She pulls them out of air and kneads them into gold.

I close my eyes until I hear a cry and the music cuts off.

Now I can hear Mr. Crowwith's voice. It is dead and musicless. "If you think you are keeping a shred of that gold—" he says, dragging the girl-Master toward the ladder. He pushes her back against it and holds his mouth very close to her jaw, as though he is going to take a bite out of her. "You stupid, stupid child. What did you think would happen? That I'd let one of my finest Masters wear a soapstress's dress sewn with bells and still keep his position?" He snatches her stone-flute from her hand and throws it behind him, into the patch of almost-dead trees. My trees.

"No!" cries the girl-Master.

But Mr. Crowwith stutters her throat with one hand, letting go only when she stops struggling. "You'll leave now before you embarrass me any further. Music doesn't belong to you any more than it belongs to them." He motions to us, the turnaway girls. Then he shoves the girl-Master again and she turns, crawling up the rungs with such tapping speed that her foot slips at the top.

"Good-bye, Linna Lundd," calls Mr. Crowwith.

"I'll deal with you when I see you next. Which I'm sure will be soon."

The girl-Master scrambles out of the skydoor, and then she's gone.

One by one, fifteen more Masters climb down from above, as though the sky itself has given them to us. They're all boys, all in jackets hemmed with bells. They play well, but none plays as beautifully as Linna Lundd did. They choose fifteen more othergirls— girls who make so much shimmer, my eyes burn as if I'm staring into fire. The air glistens as if it's been polished.

Mother Nine keeps glancing in my direction, as though she's peering at a bird hovering above my head. I try to turn my eyes to stone. She mustn't know how scared I am of staying. I try, too, not to glance at the hollow tree. At the stone-flute lying in the lungmoss.

By the time the sixteenth othergirl is chosen, the space where the Sea-Singer's heart used to be has turned blush pink with streaks of blue.

Evening has come.

The girl-Master's song still lives in my bones.

The cloisterwings tap their beaks against the bars of their cages. They're cawing and cackling for their dinner, and I wish for a second that they would eat me up—at least then I could be a part of something flying. Something singing.

I am hoping blindly now—hungrily, as the starving hope for fruit. Hoping that someone will appear. Hoping there'll be another Master. A Master to choose me. The girl-Master was sent away—maybe that means there will be another. Maybe they'll find another boy.

But this is a worthless hope. A lying hope.

Because no one will come for me. No one.

Mr. Crowwith bids Mother Nine good evening, resting his eyes on me for a moment. He opens his mouth, as if he's had a thought, but nothing slides off the surface of his tongue. He floats up the ladder toward the sky, the wind tearing at his sleeves.

Mother Nine climbs up behind him. She wrestles the door out of the wind's grip, and it slams closed over her head. The stone locks click like cracked knuckles. The rest of the othergirls sigh out breaths.

They are ready for bed. I count their heads—twenty-five of them. Twenty-five girls who will never leave the cloister. Plus one. Me.

I can hear Blightsend—bells ringing, flutes sounding. Music like spilled fire. I'll never be a part of that. I'll never leave the cloister. I have no use for my throbbing, gold-hooked ear, my stitched slippers—which are already rubbing the backs of my heels raw. I have no use for anything. All I am is a broken-boned girl who will lose all her nails, toes included, before she makes a single handful of gold. I'll never be a girl-Master in a red dress, making music as I walk.

Mother Nine tells the othergirls to go to bed. But to me she says, "Stay."

My silk-covered knees dig against the cobbles.

When the othergirls are gone, she smooths her voice and sweetens her tongue. "Delphernia—"

But she doesn't get to finish. Because that's when we hear it. Mother Nine hears it, and I hear it, and it's definitely there: it's a—

Bang.

Bang.

A knock on the rattling skydoor.

Chapter Nine

"Who's there?" says Mother Nine. She's at the top of the ladder again, tilting her ear toward the skydoor.

There's a muffled sound from behind sea-eaten wood, but it's sucked away by the wind. She must not be able to hear, because she unclicks the time-stiffened locks. The wind grabs the skydoor from her hands. I gather my skirt out of cobble-mud, getting to my feet. I peer through the skydoor, but I can only see a deep-blue and deepening sky.

"Who's there?" says Mother Nine again.

This time, a boy answers—I can hear his words if I listen carefully enough. Listening's one of the things we learn in the cloister, and not just listening with your ears, either—listening with your whole body. Listening with your bones.

"Bly," the boy says. "Bly's my name."

Mother Nine's foot slips, and I think she's about to fall back, meet Teeth Row with a crumple and snap. But she collects her limbs again, gripping the ladder.

"They say to make gold of music is to kiss the clouds," the boy continues. "Those are the First King's words. But I'm sure you know that, Ninth Mother. Obligations are kept to the sea and to kings. My name is—"

"I know," says Mother Nine. She sounds defeated. "Your name is Bly."

I don't understand why she's listening to him. She doesn't listen to anyone unless their words are written as law. Unless they're giving us food in exchange for shimmer. But she's staring through the opening of the skydoor as if there's a ghost hovering beyond it. The Ninth King's ghost.

I wait. I consider kneeling again, but I want to be ready for whoever's there—if Mother Nine lets him in, that is. I still can't see his face. The wind outside the cloister whines and hisses, slapping at stone.

Mother Nine climbs to the ground again. "Please enter," she calls.

The boy lowers himself toward Teeth Row, step by step on the creaking ladder. Lit shards of hushingstone set his face to glowing from below—brown skin and pursed lips. Black curls adorn his head. His eyes are dark.

Just like mine.

Just like the eye of the Master on the other side of the wall. The one who heard me singing. It can't be him. But it is. It is.

Don't tell, Delphernia.

The wind catches the door again and flings it shut over the boy's head. He jumps, but he keeps climbing down. And then we are held, the three of us, in the cloister's quiet: me, and Mother Nine, and a boy who could have me killed.

He approaches me, ignoring Mother Nine. His clothes are simply cut and pale, unembroidered, and his shoes are crafted out of gold. He wears no bells, but unlike Mr. Crowwith, silence doesn't follow him like a hungry mist. No—he has music in him, I can tell, and not only because of the stone-flute that's sheathed at his hip like a weapon. His hands are always moving, moving, as though he's trying to sculpt something out of air.

He looks at the trees and then lifts his eyes toward the Sea-Singer's carved portrait, which flickers in fickle light. A shadow passes over his face like a cloud covering the skydoor on a summer day — dark for a moment, then light.

I swallow the heat in my throat, looking down like a good turnaway girl.

"I've always wanted to visit this place," he says. "I watch it from the beach and I think, *Who lives there?* It's as though the stone is speaking to me. Calling me."

What is he talking about? I lace my fingers.

"Look up, please," says the boy. His voice cracks. "Eyes are two doors and they lead to the place where the soul was born."

My eyes meet his exactly. It's like someone measured him out using me as the pattern. He looks about my age, too.

"Your name?" he says.

"I'm — I'm Delphernia Undersea," I reply.

The name of a turnaway girl is like two halves of the same broken stone. The first name is what the Mother hopes for the girl. And the second is what she dreads. Mother Nine has never explained to me what *Delphernia* means, but *Undersea* is from her dictionary of failures. Under the sea. Undersea. A prophecy of drowning. What's more, a turnaway girl's name only means something to the Mother who named her. It's not meant to be used outside the dome of the cloister. But this boy seems to think my name is worth something, no matter where it's spoken.

"Yes," he says. "You will. You will follow me into the sky."

Mother Nine stomps over, her shoulders wide as walls. "But you haven't tested her," she says.

Bly looks past her. "That won't be necessary," he says. "She'll do as gold does to the palm."

I'll do—like I'm a pot or pan. The words make me scowl. But my eyes meet his again, and I take back my spite. Because he looks at me like I'm not a turnaway girl. He looks at me like I'm a person—a Master, even. Someone with a voice and words to speak with it.

"She'll be no use to you," says Mother Nine. "Your drawers will be empty of gold."

"Her usefulness will be for me and the wings of birds to decide," says Bly. A pained smile tweaks his mouth.

He looks up at the painting of the Sea-Singer again, then narrows his eyes at Mother Nine. They hold a stare between them for a long, long time. Mother Nine's jaw tightens, but she nods and takes a step back.

Then she says, "Grant me one thing. May I talk to the girl alone?"

"Words are never alone when they are spoken," says Bly. "They carry their echoes with them." But he walks back to the ladder and leans against it, watching us. Watching the cloisterwings, too.

Mother Nine crowds me with her sleeves.

"Delphernia, the safest place for you is here," she whispers, "in the cloister."

The scabs on my fingers itch. My thumb's bandage draws taut. I have to stop myself from laughing. If I don't leave the cloister now, I will live here forever. I'll be slapped until I'm nothing more than a scrap. That doesn't seem very safe to me.

Mother Nine glances up at the skydoor. "Delphernia," she says. "Trust me."

She reaches for my hand—the one with the torn thumbnail—but I rip it away. My pierced ear hums with new blood. She'll take no more skin from me.

"A Master has chosen me, Mother Nine. Hasn't

my decision already been made? Should I not walk the path I've been given?"

It's a trick of nerve, my tongue. Because she might tell me that this Master — whoever he is — is not one of the seventeen best. He's not wearing bells, after all, and Mr. Crowwith doesn't seem to know he's here. But she is as speechless as an othergirl.

I look up at the Sea-Singer. My prayer worked.

The cloisterwings shift and shuffle. My heart splits. I'll never see them again. Not if I leave. I want to run, kiss the bark of the hollow tree one last time, and brush the cloisterwings' heads with the tip of a finger. I want to tell the birds I'm sorry they'll never be free. I want to find the girl-Master's stone-flute in the lungmoss and keep it for myself.

But Bly is waiting.

"I am sorry," I whisper to the cloisterwings. The three words, so useless, are like kicks to my shin.

I do not run to the hollow tree. I ignore the whisper-room's door, like a scar in stone.

I take my stiff new dress, my hurting hand. I take my bruises. I take my voice. I walk toward the ladder.

Toward Bly.

The boy with black eyes.

The boy who knows my secret.

I climb the first worn rung behind him, watching the heels of his golden shoes scraping at salt-weakened wood.

I fill my lungs.

It's time I met the sky.

the
Old
Sorrows

Chapter Ten

I follow Bly up the ladder. Up and up. There's a long
fall below.

The only thing keeping me going is the chance to
be closer than I've ever been to the Sea-Singer. I can
almost touch one of her eyes. I hold on to the ladder with my sore hand, to brush my fingers over her
stone-etched hair.

"I'll keep you with me," I say.

Bly turns. "What was that?" he calls.

I don't answer.

For all her classes, all the things she taught us—
Histories, Silence, Making Shimmer—Mother Nine
failed to teach us one thing: how to behave around
a Master. If Bly *is* a Master. He's not one of the
best—that I know for certain. He doesn't look like
he hasn't ever heard the word *never.* He asked my

name, looked at me as though I was a girl and not a ladle with a crooked handle. And something else — he seems to understand how it feels to wear your life like a too-small coat — to know always and always and always that it's only moments from tearing. But that's only a gut-hunch. I don't know anything about him. I don't know him at all. And he doesn't know me.

Bly climbs through the skydoor and waits for me to catch up, reaching his hand through to pull me out, pull me up, pull me into —

So much shine that I struggle to swallow, choke on the night's blooming. The sea's a searing silver. The open space whirls, stretches wider. My bones turn soft as sap. Bly lets me rest against him until I find my breath again. We stand on the curved dome of the cloister, star-shimmering lungmoss under our feet. The sea crackles with cold and salt.

I can't look up again — I can't.

Instead, my eyes follow the ragged rocks sticking out above the sea's surface — a natural bridge that connects the cloister's own island to the city of music — toward my new home. But even that is too much. For a few seconds, I am stiff as a tucked quilt—as though keeping still and straight will make the world smaller. But it only expands and expands. I breathe shallow breaths. I stop breathing altogether.

"You cannot live without breathing," says Bly, gripping my unhurt hand.

I squeeze his fingers back. I breathe again—deeply, deeply—until my vision clears. "I know. I'm fine. It's—it's so beautiful." The last word sounds like a sigh. I shift my weight and straighten my dress. I'm standing underneath the sky. I'm standing on the roof of the cloister. My toes twitch, chafing against the silk of my shoes.

"Beautiful!" barks Bly. "I'd call it treacherous."

His words silence the sea. He's a Master—he must be a Master. Which means he's supposed to love Blightsend. He's supposed to pledge his music to the place. One after the other, the knobs of my spine turn to frost.

But I stop the thought that Bly might not be a Master. I close its mouth. Because there are other things to be afraid of now, and other things to embrace. Like the sound of stone-flutes and the promise of light in the distance. And the sky, which has stopped trying to choke me, which has taken up residence in my chest.

Bly drops the word *treacherous* out of his hands, digs around for a new sentence. "Even one step can take you toward the sun," he says. He's still holding my hand. My feet are limp as dead fish. "It'll be all right," he adds. "We'll take the first step together."

When I'm ready, he leads me down the stone steps that run in spirals around the cloister's dome all the way to the ground. Closer and closer to the sea's wild whistling. Closer and closer to the jagged-backed rocks that make a path toward the city. Blightsend. The name grows across my heart like a trail of lungmoss.

When we get to the first rock, our arms twist together like branches. I move my foot onto a sharp-slanted boulder, and icy water laps against my ankle, as though the sea wants a taste of me. Another step and I slide, stumble. Bly catches me against him.

"Fall not," he says. "The sea can wait."

"Wait for what?"

"Oh," he says. "I'm sorry. It's something I do when I'm nervous — quoting poems."

I think about all the odd-strung words he's spoken

this evening. Poems. The only poem I've ever read was the one written by the First Mother. We learned it in Histories.

"To live behind stone is to make a life of watching," I whisper.

Bly stops walking. His eyes strike mine. "The First Mother's poem," he says.

"Yes."

The sea is reaching its hands toward me. It wants to drag me in. The wind knocks my lungs about. My elbows snatch themselves against my ribs.

"The world is rocking," I say, pressing against Bly with my shoulder.

"I've read all the poems on the island, but I've never heard that line," he says, his brow creased.

"Oh. That's because it's not a poem. It's—a feeling."

He seems to understand.

I don't know how to talk to a boy who speaks only in the words others have written. I don't know how to talk to a boy at all.

"How old are you?" I say, taking another step, and another. "You sound like Mother Nine."

"I'm twelve," says Bly.

A wave rushes at me, foaming at my shins, giving my dress a white hem. I cover my mouth with my free hand. He could send me swimming for that disrespect. The sea backs away from me, glaring like a wide, wide eye.

Bly only twists his arm tighter around mine. "I apologize," he says. "I didn't mean to make you itch. I suppose it's because all my friends are dead men and women. Ones who wrote books a long time ago. I spend most of my time indoors."

"So you're like me," I say, feeling a pattering of warmth in my chest—a warmth that rushes against the chill of the sea. "Living behind walls?"

His eyes crease as if they've been stitched at the sides. "Your walls are of one kind," he says. "Mine are of another."

Chapter Eleven

Bly and I cross the sea together.

We cross worlds.

He doesn't let go of my arm once. I hold my chin against the sea's wild breathing. Slowly, slowly, I'm getting used to being out in the open. To having the sky see me. To seeing it all at once.

When we reach the city's edge, we untangle our elbows. My shoes of music are wet and caked with grit. There are little cuts on my ankles from slipping on stone, but my belly is warm, as though someone's made it a keeping place for freshly kneaded gold.

"Blightsend," I say, standing on the road that curves around the outskirts of the city.

I turn to Bly because I want to see Blightsend through his eyes. Want to see him seeing it. But he looks at the sky as though it's a dirty window. He peers at stone houses as though he'd rather they were rubble.

Something has caused him anguish. Something as vast as the sea and as deep as a sky full of falling stars. Because you'd have to be heart-torn to hate such a place. A city, grown of stone, on the most lonely island in the world, smooth-shining walls and slanting roofs and empty streets all strung with the chimes of bells. Shimmer dusting the windows. Tongue-fruit trees stretching their branches toward the moon. It makes me want to sing.

Don't tell.

Don't tell.

I keep my voice tucked under my tongue, smothering it with spit. My throat stays silent, but it pushes me along, into the open-flung arms of the streets. One foot and then the next. My heart gallops into quicker rhythms, and before I'm able to think of it, I'm streaking down a narrow road.

I've forgotten about the cloister, about Mother Nine. I am made only of lightness. I have no fears, no wants, nothing to dread. Not even the sky can get to me. Not even the foreverness of the sea. All my wounds quiet their aching—even my blood-dried thumb.

I sprint, smelling the city—clean cups and spun flickermoth silk. Steamed tongue-fruit and boiled seaflowers. Bowls of hushingstone bloom with fire along the pavements, lighting the way for walkers. I spread my arms, ready for flying, tearing through the gloom and the glow until I get to the center of it—to the heart of the city that beats and beats and beats.

I'm at the edge of a sunken oval, a giant shape dug into stone, a shin lower than the ground around it. It's a feather, its quill a line of three narrow steps leading down. There's a gold statue of a man, his palms raised, at the end of the quill. And there are hundreds of Masters dancing inside the feather, their clothes swarmed with golden bells. They make music just by moving. They part—two halves of a leaning forest—and a girl a little older than I am appears from within their midst. They dance around her, clapping out her name, while she stands still.

"The Childer-Queen," they chant softly. "The Childer-Queen, the Childer-Queen."

The Childer-Queen is wearing gold from head

to toe—a crown like a garden about her head and a skirt like loosed stars. Her pale silks stand out against her golden-brown skin. Her mouth is cinched like a pincushion.

Right away, I decide that she's more First Mother than Sea-Singer. Not that it matters. I'm not going anywhere near her.

There's so much beauty here, it's distracting. My eyes have never seen so many shards of hushingstone shaped like fingers, so many trays of steaming gold and glass. One of the faces halts my gazing, though. Gray eyes and ashed skin. Silence around him like a storm of flickermoths. It's Mr. Crowwith. He's standing at the tip of the giant feather. Watching.

"To live behind stone is to make a life of watching," I whisper to myself.

But Mr. Crowwith doesn't live behind walls. He has no excuse.

I step back. Back and back and back. I drift, unseen, into an unlit lane, lost in the throbbing crowd. I want to watch, but I want to hide, too.

I can't help but find the othergirls in the swell— the ones who were chosen by the best Masters. Mother Nine taught us that this dance is supposed to celebrate them, but the othergirls don't react. They stand in a row, their eyes unmoving. They are as empty as ever.

I'm still staring at the othergirls when Bly grabs my arm and yanks me toward him, splitting a seam at my shoulder. I push away, but he wraps his fingers around my wrist. My torn thumb is awake again, and I'm remembering clamps, kicks, slaps. I bare my teeth and scratch at his neck. He lets go, looking at the rip in my sleeve with regret. His mouth opens, wordless. We're surrounded by people and music, but there's a line of silence between us.

"Don't ever do that again," I say.

Bly swallows. "I have looked for gold in shadowed places and I have found only you," he says.

"What?"

"That's the Ninth King. A poem he wrote for the Sea-Singer. His statue's there, at the entrance to the Featherrut." He points through the crowd to the dancing Masters.

I fold my arms, narrow my eyes.

"I didn't mean—" he says. "I was worried. Scared. I didn't know where you'd gone. I'm sorry, Delphernia."

He takes my hand, folds my fingers into his, and

even though I'm still simmering inside, I get that feeling again: that I'm as rooted as my old hollow tree.

Before I can tell him it's all right, he taps my shoulder and says "Follow me!" And then we're twisting along glit-flitter streets speeding through the night-blue, the shimmer and shift. I've never felt so feverish, as if every vein in my body is a thin line of fire, but doubt presses at my back like a howling wind. The stone houses on either side of us dip their heads. The sky churns. All the colors forget their names.

I slow to a stop. "Aren't you going to dance?" I say. "The Festival of Bells?"

"No," he says. "No." But he doesn't explain.

He turns down a crooked street. I follow, but he's not making any sense. Masters are obliged to dance in the Festival of Bells. That's what I've been taught. I don't know what I'll do if Bly isn't really a Master. Mother Nine has not prepared me for that. Mother Nine has not prepared me for anything.

By the time we stop at a garden, the hum of Blightsend's festival like distant birds, my slippers have loosened around my skinless toes. I wince as I walk.

You'd think I'd feel at home with trees all around me. But there's something different about this garden.

Something that tugs at my sleeve but won't show its face. Moonlight reflects off the leaves, and I have to narrow my eyes because it's giving me a headache, and then I realize —

It's silent. No sounds of growing. No insect-whirrings. No birds.

Through black branches I can see a long, low building with hundreds of small windows, a central arch separating one side from the other. I pull back, but Bly urges me on through the garden's clinging.

I stop short and founder. My cheek smacks against smooth stone, a thin sheen of lungmoss. My face stings. But I stand, determined to know what it is about this garden — what it is that I can't quite grasp. Bly waits for me, watching. The sky tilts. I touch one of the leaves at my side. Its edges are sharp, its surface smooth. Smooth as metal.

And then I know where I am.

I know that every leaf, every branch, every flower, is made of gold. And I know why it's silent. This is the First King's gold-fashioned garden. The Garden of All Silences. Bly has brought me to Sorrowhall. To where the Sea-Singer sang.

The crash of the ocean fills me. A mourning song

travels on the wind. I can hear Mother Nine's voice in my head.

Girls with singing throats are swallowed by the sea.

I close my eyes.

When I open them again, Bly is still looking at me. "Weary are those who shed the skin of their old life," he says.

The garden crowds me, and I want to be calm and quiet; I want to turn Mother Nine's words to mulch, but I have to ask—

"Bly," I say, "please answer me." My teeth clatter. I wriggle my sore toes in my shoes. "Who are you? Who are you really?"

"You don't know me?" The night makes a mask of his face. "You are like me, Delphernia Undersea. I do not know myself."

"But what is your name?" I say. And my heart repeats the question. *What is your name? What is your name?*

"I am Bly Harpermall," he says. "The Prince of Blightsend."

Chapter Twelve

Hours later, I climb out of bed, slide my feet back into their slippers. I want to walk on music, want music to carry me away from here—even if it blisters my toes.

Bly—*Prince* Bly—assured me that I would soon adjust to life at Sorrowhall. This was after I started running through the hard tangle of the garden, its branches scratching my arms, my neck, my back.

Until then, I hadn't known that gardens could have claws.

Bly showed me to my sleeping-room—a small space with a stone bed and gold-carved walls, collecting dust in every gouge and hollow.

"Sleep among ghosts and you will sleep well," he said, motioning to the walls. They told some sort of story about waves and hands and mouths. Right in the center there was a tree with keys for leaves.

"Did you carve these?" I asked, running my finger along the crest of a wave.

"They're all my dreams," he said. "And my nightmares." As he left the room, he called back, "Sleep well, fellow dreamer. Sleep facing the sea. Even dreamers—"

"Must be watchful," I called back.

But sleep was not something I could accomplish.

For hours I stared at the walls, trying to understand their language. Hook-toothed vines furling into corners and trees sprouting flames. Hands with frightened eyes on their fingertips, reaching for glass-shard waves and frowning suns. My eyes were scratchy with tiredness—but I kept starting, thinking the walls had come alive. They felt alive.

They feel alive still.

I imagine them slithering closer to me, their eyes blinking like Bly's eye on the other side of the cloister's wall. I want to get out, to get away—to be anywhere but this place. Because Bly is wrong. I won't adjust to life at Sorrowhall—not if I can't make shimmer. He'll soon know that I can't. And if I disappoint him, he'll tell the Childer-Queen he heard me singing. He will. He will.

The sea will find me on its tongue soon enough.

I wrestle with the musty quilt, wrap it around me to hide my turnaway dress. I slip the case off its pillow and fold it into a strip, tying it over my forehead and ears to hide my turnaway piercing. My ear is so tender that I have to bite my tongue when the silk touches it. I cannot handle pain—certainly not well enough for someone who flouts every known law in Blightsend.

Mother Nine would say I am a cowardly criminal.

I creep out into the wide passageway, my dress and the gilded edge of the quilt trailing a path through dirt.

The Garden of All Silences is a strange, sad thing—a garden that does not grow. A garden must have life in it to be one. My forest inside the cloister might have been almost-dead, but at least it had the beating of wings, the soil-churn of mudworms, the flit and shimmer of flickermoths.

I didn't even say good-bye to the cloisterwings, and now I will never see them again. They will wither and die inside the cloister, caged by Mother Nine. They will never know what it is to crease the sky with their wings.

Wings—the wind lifts at the word, tearing at angles to rip the quilt from around me.

And I run, I run.

The city's streets are deserted, but I still step awkwardly, avoiding rhythms. In case someone's listening. In case someone's watching.

I thought Blightsend would take me into its hands and stroke my head, but even here there's no safe place for me. The sky's always glaring. The sea rushes, rushes. I struggle against a wall of wind.

I want to escape. To find a way to leave. But one look at the boundless gray that surrounds the island is all I need to know that isn't possible—not even a little, not even in dreams.

I walk, trying to ignore the gnaw in my heart, until I get to the edge of the Featherrut. I follow the curve of it until I reach the steps and the statue of the bent-necked man—arms outstretched, palms to sky. Flickermoths twirl around him. There's a little plaque at the statue's base that says:

RULLUN HARPERMALL
THE NINTH KING

The wind dies down, turning to a hushing waft.

The flickermoths drift off, and the sea flattens out like a stretched sheet of silk. I watch abandoned bells rolling across the bottom of the Featherrut, jingling faintly so that what's left of the wind—a gentle breeze—sounds like it's wearing Master-garb.

Then I see a girl.

She's thin as cut shadow, staring at me with her chin cocked. Her skin is white as stars. She's wearing a soapstress's dress—silk dyed with the red juice of tongue-fruit. A silent jacket swamps her shoulders.

She unsticks her lips. I rearrange my quilt, trying to hide my turnaway dress, and start to walk away. But her footsteps follow me—light footsteps, as though she's tripping across a sheltered strait on the smooth backs of rocks, her stone heels tapping musically against the ground.

"Wait!" she calls.

I stop, turning toward the shadow-girl—hoping she will be quiet.

The wind lifts again. The moon hits the soapstress's face and it's—it's *her*. The girl-Master, whose dress, only hours ago, was sewn with hundreds of golden bells. The girl who played her stone-flute so beautifully that Mr. Crowwith threw it to the lungmoss.

"I'm sorry—I didn't mean to frighten you," she says.

"I'm not frightened," I say, but I start walking again, toward Sorrowhall—to my place, as Mother Nine would say.

I'll sleep in the garden if I have to, to avoid those creep-pressing walls. I'll sleep in the place where the Sea-Singer sang and pretend her song still lives there, spun among the branches of bent-gold trees like an eight-legger's web. I cannot afford to break more rules. More than that, I cannot afford to have another person witness me breaking them.

The girl-Master trots alongside me, extending a hand. "I'm Linna," she says. "Linna Lundd."

"I know. You announced your own name in the cloister."

"Only because Mr. Crowwith would've said it wrong."

This makes me stop. "What do you mean?"

"I had a different name before. Before I chose a new one for myself. Before I chose one that was true. Do you like it?"

I love it. It's like two sung notes—perfect for a

girl who can play the stone-flute like she can. But I don't say that. I look down and nod.

"What do you mean — true?" I ask.

"A name must fit a person like the right size shoe. Mine didn't, before. So I changed it."

For a thousand seconds, I do not know what to do with my eyes, my hands, my feet.

"I didn't rescue your stone-flute," I say. "I'm sorry."

Cowards are not supposed to admit to their cowardice. I know that. But there's something about Linna that makes me feel calm, as if I could go to sleep at her feet, not worry about being kicked.

She shrugs. "I'm taking it as a sign from the sky," she says, smiling widely. "No music for a little while."

"It was lying there, and I — I could have. But he — the Master. He was waiting, and—"

"Can you play?" Linna asks.

I shake my head frantically. "Of course not."

Linna is smiling again — for no reason — and her smile is louder than any music I've ever heard. I remember the music she played in the cloister, and my bones start rushing with the notes.

There's an ache inside me that's hunger and also

not hunger: an emptiness of the heart. I don't want to return to that room of dust, don't want to sit in the Garden of All Silences. The Sea-Singer might have sung there, but the Sea-Singer was swallowed by the sea.

I can't help but glance at Linna's dress again.

"What happened to the bells?"

"Oh, that was a costume I made for the Festival. But it seemed wiser, after Mr. Crowwith spat his threats, to wear more silent attire." She pronounces the words as the Custodian would, full of mocking seriousness, then flings her arms open and dances a triplet of steps across stone. Her palms are dusted with gold.

"Are you in hiding? Where will you live?" I call. My heart does its own frightened waltz. Everything Mother Nine's told me says that there's no space in Blightsend for those who don't fit like the right key for the right lock. And Linna—girl-Master and soapstress—doesn't fit.

Like a shimmerless turnaway girl.

Linna pirouettes back. "I've already told you a few secrets and you haven't told me any of yours," she says, straightening her shoulders. "Haven't you heard the saying? Secrets must be exchanged, not given. A secret for a secret. Otherwise someone'll go telling." She raises an eyebrow.

I blink at her.

Then she shrugs and whispers against my cheek, as though she can't resist. "I won't tell you where, but I will tell you this: I live in a cloister of my own."

"A cloister?" My throat feels full of the word.

"You're horrified," she says, laughing again.

I can't stop myself from laughing with her. I'm surprised by the music of it: two voices becoming one. But I brush the thought away. I can't risk making music with anyone. I can't risk making music at all. I'm not like Linna. I'm not a girl-Master. I could never wear a dress sewn with bells.

Linna's eyes are full of light—it's as though she's siphoned off moonlight to make her irises. I can't picture this girl in a cloister, even if it is one she built for herself. She is made of the ringing sky. She is made of a thousand bells, all strung against red silk.

"I don't understand," I say. "Are you still one of Blightsend's best Masters? I mean, you must have been, right? You were invited to the cloister to choose a turnaway girl."

"I was. But I'm not anymore. You heard what Mr. Crowwith said. Music doesn't belong to me anymore—all because I'm wearing a dress." She snorts, then sighs. "The sad thing is, it's not like I don't want to make music. But I couldn't be a Master and be me at the same time."

She says the words—*couldn't be a Master and be me*—as if they're poisonous, but I can think of worse things. Worse words. Words like *swallowed by the sea*. Words like *gone* and *dead*.

"Besides," she continues, "I wanted to make shimmer, too. Like you. Like the turnaway girls. So I taught myself how. The First Mother said—"

"Why would you care what the First Mother said?" I say, surprised by my own words.

This makes Linna close her mouth.

I unwind the bandage from my thumb, show her the raw flesh.

She hovers her hand over it, doesn't touch. "What happened?" she whispers.

"Mother Nine. With a wooden clamp." I picture the First Mother's eyes flickering, lit by lanterns in the whisper-room. "Mother Nine, the First Mother— they're all the same."

"But the First Mother didn't—she never would've—"

Hearing Linna defend the First Mother when she never had to sit under her gaze in the whisper-room fills my throat with fire. "Never would've what?" I tie the bandage around my thumb again.

"She'd never have hurt someone," says Linna. "The First Mother wrote that anyone could make shimmer. She believed in equality, freedom—"

The words rattle at stone. Blightsend is folding in on me. Its leaning houses turn into waves that tower and twist and shatter and dip.

I cover my head with my hands.

"Are you all right?" says Linna. "You look ill."

There's stone all around me like the rising dead, spinning and circling, and a sky that's laughing with a star-scattered tongue. The sea is a twisting pit of severed wings. Of course I'm ill.

I turn from her, and the wind protests, pulling at my dress and the quilt at my shoulders, spinning gold pins from my hair. The wind's been kneading at my bun since I left the cloister, and now half-plaited curls dance at my back.

I run, trying not to think about how, for the first

time ever, I feel as though I have met someone whose soul-shape matches mine. A heart-gale batters my insides. I'll probably never see her again. I shouldn't. I've already broken so many rules. The wind hisses at my ankles.

"Wait," says Linna. "Wait."

But I don't look back.

Chapter Thirteen

Morning fills my sleeping-room with brilliant shrieks of light. I watch the walls, hoping there's something I didn't see before—a piece that makes all the pictures fit together. But the twisting patterns only twist more, muddling my vision. I blink until my eyes clear.

And then I hear the stone-flute.

I follow the sound and find Bly in a dust-coated room.

The ceilings and walls are covered in dirt-edged gold—gold that has been carved with images. Gardens flooded with jagged waves, books with keys dangling from their pages, girls with flaming lungs.

Hanging on the gold-carved walls are rectangles of polished stone with portraits carved into them.

Cold settles at my neck like a scarf.

They remind me of the portraits of the Mothers in the whisper-room. But these show men and boys holding stone-flutes, women with their hands in their laps, their dresses swallowing them in folds of white silk the way water swirls about rocks. There's even a portrait of the Sea-Singer. I recognize her—painted black eyes filled with fight. Her belly is round as a full moon. Beside her, a tiny Childer-Queen stands, her hair adorned with seaflowers. The portrait must have been carved shortly before the Sea-Singer sang in the Garden of All Silences.

I turn to Bly.

He's sitting on a scuff-cracked chair, playing a rambling, quick-footed song. He hasn't looked up since I walked in. It's as though the music is holding its hands over his eyes.

I sit down on a flickermoth-eaten cushion. A filigree of dust blooms around me and settles again before Bly flicks his eyes up to meet mine.

"Oh," he says, embarrassed. "I didn't see you." He lowers his stone-flute.

I clear my throat. "Good morning, Prince Harpermall."

"I have many names, but that one I hate the most," says Bly. "I see you found the clothes I left out for you."

"Yes," I say, feeling as though all the carved faces on the walls have turned their eyes toward me at the same time. I'm wearing a shirt that is softer than my own scrubbed skin. It buttons at the back instead of the front, and it took me forever to bend into it. Then there are trousers and a thick silk jacket with cuffs that ripple like the crests of waves.

It's strange to be wearing trousers and a jacket. Even stranger to be wearing pale silks. But it's a comfort, too. I'm dressed like Bly—though my clothes have swirls of embroidery on them, and his are plain as clouded heaven. I want to feel that this is a kinship, but Mother Nine's voice is in my head, pounding like a fist against a door, saying that it's only Bly's way of reminding me that I'm different from the othergirls.

That he knows I sing.

I won't, I won't. I won't lift my voice. Ever. I will hide my desire for music like a cloisterwing sitting on her egg.

There's a bowl of tongue-fruit at Bly's feet. I reach for one, unthinking—I hate tongue-fruit, but I'm starving—when Bly lifts a hand.

"Wait," he says, and Linna's voice fills my mind: *Wait, wait, wait.* I can't imagine her in a cloister. I picture her dancing under stars. I picture me dancing with her — singing, too. Making a glow in night air. Feeling like a tree among trees.

"There's a tradition," says Bly.

Linna evaporates.

"A tradition?"

Bly places his stone-flute in an open case and stands. I can't help but stare at the instrument. It's carved out of hushingstone and etched with the wings of flying birds, its keys a line of curling waves. I think of Linna's stone-flute. I should have picked it up. Should have taken it with me. But music doesn't belong to me. Never has. Never will.

Bly takes a tongue-fruit from the bowl. He tears it in half. The red juice drips on the floor, mixing with dust. He squeezes some into his palm, motions that he'd like to do the same for me.

I hold out my hand — the one without the bandage. I do not want to think of blood, but the juice runs along creases, making a crooked *M* in my palm as though someone's sliced the skin, and then I am standing on Teeth Row again, and Mother Nine is coming with her wooden clamp —

"A licked palm is a token of surrender," says Bly. His words draw me back into the room of faces. "I will keep no secrets from you as long as you don't keep any from me." He licks his own palm, nods at me to do the same.

I can't promise that. Even if he's already heard me sing.

But I lower my eyes and suck the juice off my skin. My palm tastes of salt.

Bly hands me both halves of the tongue-fruit, then sits again and lifts his stone-flute carefully from its bed. He begins to play. I've always thought music is what it sounds like to ask the world a question. But Bly's music sounds more like a telling—like he's telling a story about all that he's lost.

The eyes of Blightsend's kings and queens prickle my cheeks.

I turn to glance at the Sea-Singer again. I whisper a prayer to her. A short prayer. One word: "Please."

A clatter. I turn to Bly. He's let his stone-flute fall to the ground.

"I'm sorry," he says, picking up the instrument.

"What is it?" I say.

"I told you I wouldn't keep secrets," he says. "Delphernia?"

"Yes?"

"There's something I want to show you."

Chapter Fourteen

It's impossible for me to think of the ocean as anything but alive. It shifts under rain like the back of a beast. The beach is rocky, laden with splinters of black hushingstone. Boulders that look like giants with bent necks line the shore.

As we step onto the sloped fall of stone, something in me spirals and cracks. The sky wears its clouds like a frowning brow. The ocean spits. I grasp at air.

I do not know how anyone ever gets used to the width of the sky.

"It's all right," says Bly, locking his elbow with mine the way he did on the day we met. Yesterday — that was yesterday.

I can't move. All I want to do is stand very still, right here, holding on to Bly and not going anywhere — ever.

"Where are you taking me?" I ask.

"It's not too far," he says, pointing.

My eyes follow to where the strip of beach tapers to meet a steep cliff. Caves howl there like open mouths. It'll be lightless and damp inside one of them, but at least I'll have a roof over my head. I'll be hidden from the sky. I'll be hidden from the sea.

"All right," I say. "Slowly."

"Slowly," Bly echoes.

The caves are even more horrid up close, smelling of salt and rotten seaflowers. Bly slips his arm out from under mine and steps inside the largest one. In moments, he's gone — swallowed.

I follow him, relieved to be in shadow.

A few times I skid on slick rock, glad to be wearing boots of stone and silk instead of slippers — even if they press against my blisters as if Mother Nine has instructed them to. I keep on, and then, just when I think I can't forge forward any longer, Bly reaches back and takes my hand.

He walks through dark the way birds fly through air.

Up ahead, a beaming light flits and crimps. Bly strikes a slice of hushingstone against the cave's wall and uses it to breathe the lamps—little gold chambers nailed into place and filled with flaming stone—into flickering. And that's when I see the faces—hundreds of them. Stone sculptures have been carved out of the cave's walls. Boys with wings for hands and clawed beasts with fishes' scales. Birds, too—small ones, their wings spread out, stilled in graceful motion. I quiver as we walk, imagining mouths opening to swallow me, taloned hands reaching to scratch at skin. We're getting closer to the glow in the distance, but I still can't see what it is.

"What's that light?" I say. My heart trips ahead of me.

Bly doesn't answer for a long while. He says "You'll see" only when I *do* see—when I'm right up close to the light and I know that it's one of the golden birds I made in the cloister.

Its wings beat against the curve of glass.

Glass—so that there's no gap to squeeze through.

So that it can't escape.

It's trapped inside a round enclosure that sits on twisted stone legs.

My chest tightens. I wanted to hide from the sky, but suddenly the cave seems smaller and smaller. As small as a globe of glass that could keep even a light-winged bird from flying.

Bly caught the bird after I sang it alive. Bly has proof of me breaking the law.

The rush of the sea fills my ears. I can feel the beating of the little bird's wings as though they're beneath my skin. Rage flares in my throat. It's *my* bird—mine. I don't want a part of me caged. But it's something else, too. It's a mark of guilt.

My death, wearing feathers.

Girls with singing throats are swallowed by the sea.

I want to run. But I cannot run. So I make my feet into liars. I promised I wouldn't hide anything, but I hide myself. I let my eyes go still and blank. I have seen enough turnaway faces to know how to look as though I'm disappearing.

Bly steps up to the glass enclosure and holds his palm against it. The bird shivers its panicked wings.

I fold my tongue in my mouth. Fear forms a seam between my lips. The Prince seems to be waiting.

"It's beautiful," I say, once I'm sure I can speak without breathlessness.

My voice doesn't sound like me at all. It sounds like the voice of a girl made of stone—as though I am one of Bly's sculptures. Light dips, surges again, and the sculptures look as though they are moving—crawling straight out of the walls. I look away, focus on the bird. I step closer to the glass. The little thing tilts its head at me—as though it remembers. My eyes fill with tears.

Bly sits down on a mound of rock. I notice that he has not brought his stone-flute with him. Relief seeps through my kneecaps. He won't ask me to make shimmer—not here. Not yet.

"You know," says Bly, "everyone thinks that Blightman Harpermall founded this place as a haven for musicians. But that's not true. At least it's not the whole truth. Blightsend was started for gold. The royal family is rich because of the turnaway girls—and all because Blightman Harpermall needed to prove something to the home that would not have him."

I do not like the way he is speaking. As though I am not one of the turnaway girls. As if the Childer-Queen is not his sister. "We each have our place," I say, stroking the glass with the tips of my fingers. "And it does not bother a turnaway girl to do her work." I try not to cringe. I sound so much like Mother Nine.

I flatten a hand against the glass. The golden bird's wings are warm behind it. It struggles, bumping at the scratched surface. But it can't get free. Bly stares at its frantic wings. I can't decide whether he looks like he wants to nail it down or set it free.

"There is not enough time in the world for birds," he says. "The First Mother said that. I think she meant that no matter how much time we have, we will never truly understand them."

"But she made them," I say, forgetting I'm supposed to be turnaway-like. "She must have understood them."

"She understood what it was to be caged."

I pull my hand away from the glass and turn to look at him.

"You know the story, Delphernia."

"What story?"

"Blightman Harpermall and Pahliah Paradi," says Bly. When he sees the blank look on my face, he continues. "The First King and the First Mother. They ran away together. From a land where art was hated—where creativity was seen as evil. He was a musician. A flautist. She was a sculptor. They found this island after eight hundred days at sea. They ate tongue-fruit and filled their mouths with rain. Pahliah carved Blightman a flute out of hushingstone, since his first one had been destroyed when they fled their home. She asked him to play for her. That's when she realized she could turn his music into gold—*real* gold—by letting it run through her bones, pulling it out of air and kneading it. As soon as Blightman saw this, he started building the cloister. He told her he was building a place for them to live. And when it was done, he locked her inside it. He left the island, traveled the outerworlds to find talented musicians—Masters. And girls for the First Mother to train. The first turnaway girls. He promised them all the gold they could possibly imagine. He brought them back with him and he set his ship on fire. And that's how Blightsend began."

We didn't learn about this in Histories. Mother Nine is stingy with her secrets, after all.

"It's time to go," says Bly.

There's an edge to his voice—a rasp like metal against stone. This has been a test. He wanted to see if I would tell him the truth about the bird. And I have failed.

"But we've only been here a little while," I say.

I don't want to leave the bird. It is a part of me. And I want to know more about Blightsend. I want to know about everything.

"But you'll be late," says Bly. "You'll be late. Late, late."

The frustration is gone from his throat now. All I hear is tiredness, as though he wants to sleep for three hundred years instead of being in a cave with me. And my lies. And tales of Blightsend's first hateful king.

I turn my head. "Late for what?" I say.

"To meet the Childer-Queen." He looks at the ground and then back at me. "And so you're forewarned—her eyes see all."

I hold a hand to the golden bird's glass cage one

last time. "That doesn't bother me," I say. "I don't have anything to hide." The bird presses its light to my palm. Heat runs through me.

"Even the dead have secrets," says Bly, blowing out the lamps as he walks.

Chapter Fifteen

The Childer-Queen is seated on a throne at the edge of a cliff, the pale sea rushing behind her like a veil. Her back is straight. Her nails are sharp. A jagged little crown sits on her head. Her eyes are a bright golden brown, but I imagine her skin would be cold to the touch. She looks a little like the Sea-Singer, only sharper, as though her mother made her from glass.

Sorrowhall looms at her side, and the Garden of All Silences is like a pool of molten gold behind us. The sky is clear as an eye.

We're all here, at the cliffs, to meet her. Me and the sixteen othergirls. And Bly, who stands beside me as if he's trying to shield me from an approaching storm — a storm only he can see coming. His face is so close to mine that I can feel his jaw clenching and unclenching against my cheek.

I watch the Childer-Queen.

"Why's she called the Childer-Queen?" I whisper, unable to tear my eyes from her angled face.

"Well, she's a child," says Bly. "And she's queen." He shrugs. "Her fourteenth birthday has only just passed."

"And why's she sitting so close to the cliff?" I'm shivering, thinking of it. The steep fall. The rocks below.

"It's a ritual Mr. Crowwith devised. The Ninth King used to do it, too. It's supposed to show the monarch as blameless—so blameless, the sea wouldn't even think of stealing them."

"But what about—even sleepers—?"

"Must be watchful, yes." Bly shifts away, and I meet his eyes. "That's because no one's ever blameless in their sleep. Sleep is when secrets stir."

I look down at my hands, struggle for a word to change the tide of conversation. "Mother Nine called her strong," I suggest.

Bly smirks. "She's determined to continue our father's legacy of laws—that's the truth. To make sure all girls stay musicless. If I were you, I'd keep my distance and stay invisible."

My mouth is dry, as though it's been stuffed with fallen leaves. He knows that it was me who sang. He does, he does, he does. But he isn't telling. He must want something from me.

I hope it's something I can give.

I hope it isn't shimmer.

"Are you close to her?" I ask, trying to stop my thoughts from growing a garden of despair in my chest.

"We've been separated since I was born. I live in the Old Sorrows — the eastern wing of Sorrowhall — and she was raised in the western wing, the New Sorrows, under the guidance of Mr. Crowwith. I was passed from nurse to nurse, left to my own education in the Sea-Singer's library, while the Childer was educated by the Custodian." He sighs. "My tongue might be slippery, but the Childer-Queen and the Custodian — their tongues have hooks."

"Hooks?"

Bly lowers his voice. "Mr. Crowwith was born without music. Everywhere he went, silence followed him like an enveloping shadow. He could never be a Master, so he used his silence to gain power—he started spying. And he found that if he listened close enough, everyone had a secret. Even the King's closest advisers. One by one, he turned the King against all of them. Until he was alone. The position of Custodian didn't even exist until Mr. Crowwith came about. He invented it, though now he acts like the post has never not been a part of Blightsend's Histories. And he is always speaking into the Childer-Queen's ear."

"He turned her against you."

"He didn't even give us a chance to be brother and sister. He's raised her on his ideas, and I don't think she knows any different. He taught her to hate me. And my mother. He taught everyone to hate my mother."

Bly doesn't belong here, either. Like Linna. Like me.

I stare at the Childer-Queen again. She's beautiful—in the way of stone knives with gold-carved hilts. When she speaks, it's difficult for me not to imagine her teeth as gleaming needles.

"Turnaway girls," she says, opening her arms, "welcome to the Festival of Kisses. It is customary for each released turnaway girl to kiss her monarch's hand. It's the grace of Lull Harpermall that has freed you, after all."

I turn back to Bly, but he's vanished.

The sea whistles, as if to remind me of its presence. The ground sinks and lifts under my feet. Without Bly to hold on to, I lean to the right, topple, crouch on the ground. My thumb throbs.

Then I remember Bly's words. If I can't grasp his arm, I can hold on to them. I try to recall the ones he spoke in the cave. *Blightsend was started for gold. The royal family is rich because of the turnaway girls. Without us, this great city would crumble and fall into the sea.*

"Without us," I whisper. "Without us." I repeat the phrase until my shins have stopped wobbling. Until I can stand again.

I'm beginning to imagine Blightsend's descent—the slow-cracking stone, the rushing waves, the statue of Rullun Harpermall sinking like an old relic to the ocean floor—when Mr. Crowwith appears, his silence louder than a slammed door. He stands before the Childer-Queen, obscuring her light.

"Mr. Crowwith," says the Childer-Queen, shifting on her throne. "Good afternoon. We were about to begin with the kisses."

He moves to her side.

It's Mr. Crowwith who signals one of the othergirls, flicking his chin at her. She approaches the throne, bending to kiss the Childer-Queen's gold-ringed hand. But the Childer-Queen's eyes skim over the top of her head, studying our faces.

The sea inches its way closer to me.

"Without us," I whisper. "Without us." It's an odd chant, but it keeps my mind on one thing: Mother Nine told us we were nothing, but we are important. *I* am important, even if I can't make shimmer. I remember the weight of the golden bird in my hand. I can make life.

Mr. Crowwith points his spear of a chin at me.

I walk toward the Childer-Queen. She extends her left hand. I bend my head, touch fingers to lips, then I kiss her scarless knuckles, my nose brushing the gold-and-stone rings that decorate her fingers.

Her whisper is so quick, so delicate—like a flicker-moth shifting under my clothes—that I nearly do not hear it.

But I do hear it.

I smell it, too.

Her breath smells of ripe tongue-fruit.

"What's your name?"

I look up. The roots of her eyelashes are golden. My tongue stops working, and it's a long stomp of seconds until I stammer out the syllables and stagger back under the cloud-blackened sky.

The Childer-Queen straightens her pale gold-stitched sleeves, readies herself to receive the next othergirl.

I watch her.

She seems always to be glancing somewhere behind me — at the tangled garden that looms there, all twisted branch and unrustling leaf.

No one is supposed to ask the name of a turn-away girl — let alone a monarch.

She knows something. I try to keep a grip on my chant, to remember that without us Blightsend would be nothing, but it comes out warped and the wind steals it.

Far away, I can hear crying — sobs and lullabies. It sounds like a woman singing. It sounds like she's singing a mourning song. But no one would do that.

Not since the Sea-Singer was taken into the ocean's mouth for disobeying.

"Without us," I say, my tongue going numb. "Without us. Without us." But the words don't work anymore. My thumb is pulsing again, as if to remind me of pain.

This is what you're in for, Delphernia.

Bly might be a poem-speaking prince, but I am a worse animal. I am a shimmerless turnaway girl with a brain as crowded as a cloisterwing cage.

Don't tell.

I shush my thoughts.

There — that sound again.

A howl on the howling wind.

Chapter Sixteen

After the kisses, the Childer-Queen motions to the garden behind us, every dangling leaf and arched branch glinting in the light that filters through the gathering clouds.

"You may wander about the First King's golden garden," she says. The sea raises its head. "But remember: it's a silent place. No sound allowed. Not even whispers."

Silent or singing, I don't want to walk among the dead-gold flowers. But I also don't want to stand out any more than I already do.

As the othergirls move toward the shine of curlicued leaves, I get to my feet, closing my eyes. I stumble, reach for branches when I get to the garden's border. The glare's pounding my head.

I could not wander about even if my feet would

let me. I'm too worried to walk—worried that the Childer-Queen knows my name, knows my list of sins. Worried that the sea will know them soon, too.

The sky's resting on my eyelids, clouds pressing down on my brow. I peer back to see the cliff's edge, trying to avoid looking up at the glowering heavens. It's like not being able to look away from a nest-fallen egg. My stomach shrinks and my lungs shrivel and I try to close my eyes—

But I can't.

The rocks below, the sea sweeping around them.

A *whoosh* of wind pulls all the air out of my chest. I clutch at a tree, lean against it, faltering into the webbing of branches. Into the garden. And then I'm surrounded by the soundless glistening of gold.

"Afraid of heights?"

I turn, startled.

The Childer-Queen herself said we shouldn't speak in the garden. But it's her. Speaking to me.

"It's all right," she says, holding a finger to her lips. "I won't tell anyone if you don't."

"I'm not afraid," I whisper, barely audible even to myself. I would never tell anyone what frightened me. Especially not a foe.

"I didn't know Bly was going to take a turnaway girl until I saw him talking to you today." She glances about to check that no one's spying her lips. Her eyes flicker. "It's all perfectly lawful, of course, insofar as the Prince of Blightsend can do what he likes—as long as the Custodian isn't bothered, which he rarely is when it comes to Bly. He doesn't think much of my brother."

I stare at the words dripping out of her mouth.

"All I'm saying is," she says, "we're family now." She steps closer to me, lifting my chin with her knuckle. One of her rings digs into my gullet. "Is he taking good care of you in the Old Sorrows?" she asks. "Can you breathe for all the dust?"

I nod. Bly might have my golden bird in a cage, but I'm more free than I've ever been. He may have heard me singing, but I don't think he's going to tell anyone about that. At least—I hope he won't. I hope he won't. I hope he won't.

All at once, the sky empties itself of rain. Drops clatter like little stones. I'm still holding on to the tree beside me, leafy fruits dangling from its branches in the wind.

But the Childer-Queen throws her head back and

stretches out her tongue. She fills her mouth with rain. If you took away her rings and crown, she could be a girl like me.

Don't tell, Delphernia.

The rain falls heavier and heavier.

The othergirls flock to stand beneath a tall tree, bark-patterns etched into the gold, branches spread out like a vaulted ceiling. I follow them reluctantly, not wanting to draw attention to myself. Up close, I can see that each of the huge tree's leaves is a glinting key. A host of secrets chimes the air. The rain stops. Droplets sit on every surface, mirroring—and shattering—the sky.

Then the Childer-Queen joins us beneath the thick gold branches. She's drenched. Strands of sopping hair cling to her cheeks.

I'm beginning to think that she might laugh— that we might all end up rolling on the lungmossy ground, tearing in gasps between roared guffaws— when Mr. Crowwith appears behind her. As if his silence has scolded her, she straightens her sleeves.

She must feel the fever of my staring, because she turns to stare right back, watches as I shift uncomfortably in my bruised skin, my blister-giving shoes.

The cliffs hum my name. The ocean steams.

I want to tear my eyes away, but there's too much space outside the cage of the Childer-Queen's gazing. Everything's buzzing like a trapped flickermoth—except the Childer-Queen. If I blink, I will turn to dust.

She walks up to me, eyes unyielding, and takes my hand. Her fingers are cold with rain.

She smiles as though she has a secret.

Or as though she knows one.

Hiddenhall

Chapter Seventeen

I can taste the sea all the time.

The wind leaves a layer of salt on my lips, and my eyelashes are flecked with little crystals. They're like old tears, reminding me how close I am to drowning. Reminding me what happens to girls like me.

Girls with singing throats.

It's been five days since I left the cloister, and Bly hasn't asked me to make shimmer. And he hasn't mentioned the golden bird since he took me to his cave.

The sea still spins me into dizziness if I don't plant my feet. But I mustn't dread the sky. I mustn't let Mother Nine win. She said it would be worse for me out here, but nothing can be worse than being trapped in the cloister—not even being dragged into jaw-jagged waves. I do not want to believe her words and so I will make them untrue. I will keep the laws of Blightsend. I won't even think about singing.

Especially not on the Festival of the Sea-Singer.

I am standing on the black, black beach, surrounded by lanterns—gold cages paneled with glass and filled with pieces of hushingstone. The crowds of Masters sound like building storms, their bells a resounding chorus. You can hear them from afar—not like Mr. Crowwith. It could be a spoonful of useful, that bell sound, if you wanted to escape this place, keep an ear out for following feet. If there were somewhere to escape to, that is.

"I will keep the laws of Blightsend," I whisper. "And they will keep me."

At least I have the festival to distract me.

In Blightsend, each day wears a different dress. The Festival of Bells, the Festival of Kisses.

Yesterday was the Festival of Fingers. All day, Masters gathered at the Featherrut to trill scales and see who could play the longest songs without breathing. They feasted on thumb-shaped biscuits dipped in sweet tongue-leaf tea.

The day before was the Festival of Skies, which didn't mean anything, really, except that you were meant to look up and be grateful. The beach was filled with Masters, lying on their backs, staring up as if trying to decipher the language of clouds.

The Childer-Queen arrives at the Festival of the Sea-Singer with Mr. Crowwith at her side, the train of her mist-wafting dress collecting small, sea-smoothed pebbles of hushingstone. She releases red ribbons of silk, obviously dyed with tongue-fruit juice, into the churning wind. They look like bloodied bandages.

The ribbons are gathered by Masters and wives, soapstresses, even turnaway girls. They're wound around fingers, tied around necks. Fished out of the sea, dripping. They are supposed to be tongues. It was the Sea-Singer's tongue that got her swallowed, after all—sent the waves to pull her from her bed.

I know the festival is supposed to be a celebration of her death, but I will not celebrate that. I will celebrate the fight I saw in her eyes, in the cloister and in the Old Sorrows.

Capes of cloud sweep the horizon, and the sea spits and shivers with the spines of waves. I try not to look at the ribbons, try not to imagine them bloody. Try not to think about those clouds reaching down with frayed fingers to snatch me from my feet—

"There you are!"

I jump, turn. It's Linna, wearing a silent soap-stress's dress. Her cheeks are pink, as if she's been running.

"Good evening," I say.

I watch her taking in the festival: the sour smell of tongue-fruit wine, the drenched ribbons rippling on the surface of the sea. The music spinning from stone-flutes like unraveling spools of fire-lit thread. Masters are sticking out their tongues, miming drowning, laughing themselves sick, while soapstresses fill their palms with sea foam. Wives are dressed in layers of silk dyed with seaflower petals, their sleeves stitched with gold, their eyes eclipses of boredom. Turnaway girls drift between them, staring at the horizon as though it's another stone wall. I wonder if anyone ever thinks about who the Sea-Singer really was. She isn't only a story to worry children with at night.

"Aren't you afraid Mr. Crowwith will see you?" I say to Linna. But I am smiling. Because you can't look at this girl and not smile — and not have hope.

"I'm dressed the part," she says, taking a small tongue-fruit out of her skirt's pocket and handing it to me. "And I'll keep my distance from him." She hesitates, peering over my shoulder. Then she whispers, "You know you're being watched, though, right?"

I glance behind me to see the Childer-Queen staring. "I don't think I'm supposed to be here alone," I say. "But my Master doesn't exactly like Festivals."

The truth is, Sorrowhall twists me into knots. I don't want to sit in my dust-gold sleeping-room, waiting for Bly to ask for my company. He's gone most days—in that cave of his. Carving eyes and hands, teeth and claws and hooked beaks. And keeping a little golden bird behind glass.

"Your Master isn't here?" says Linna.

"No." A wave swells with ribbon-tongues at my side. My stomach fills with the wings of frightened birds. I still don't know why he hasn't asked me to make shimmer. I still don't know why he has my golden bird—or if he's ever going to tell me outright that he knows it's mine. "He hardly leaves the Old Sorrows."

Linna narrows her eyes. "Wait. You're the Prince's turnaway girl?"

My face turns hot.

"You have to tell me about him," she says, smiling and grasping my shoulders. "Is he really as odd as they say? Odd people are the best."

I can't help it—I look at her and a laugh escapes me. Mother Nine's eyes always made me feel as though my hands were the size of dinner plates. I felt clunky under her gaze, like I was cobbled together out of found things. Like my own teeth didn't fit inside my mouth. But not with Linna.

"I mean, I suppose he's a little odd," I say. "He's always quoting poems."

Linna's expression crumples like a squashed sea-flower. "That's not that odd," she says, clearly disappointed.

I laugh again. I've never laughed so much in my life. Twice. In one evening. I wonder if the sky's heard me. I try to look up, but a rushing of nausea surges up from my toes. I stare at the ground, suck my tongue until it passes.

Linna's still looking at me expectantly.

"Fine—I can say this," I whisper. "He has a cave. And he's carved all these enormous beasts out of the walls, and they almost look—they almost look alive."

"Alive!" Linna cries. "Now, that's something I can work with." She grabs the fruit from my hand, shrugs, and takes a bite. "If you're not going to eat it," she says, mouth full.

"But really, he's quite ordinary." I roll a pebble over with my toe. "He's just a person who likes to stay indoors."

"Right," says Linna, her tongue stained dark red. "Well, if I lived at Sorrowhall, I'd stay indoors, too, to be honest."

I don't mention that the Old Sorrows is falling apart. I don't mention that it has more flickermoths than servants. I don't mention that I am always alone there, trying to unhear the faint singing that comes from the Garden of All Silences when the wind is pitched right.

As if she can hear that haunting sound herself, Linna says, "I need to go." She must catch the *don't-leave* look in my eye, because she adds, "But if you'd like to see *my* cloister—meet me at the statue of Rullun Harpermall later?"

"All right," I say, wanting to go but knowing I shouldn't. Especially if Bly suspects me for singing. Especially if the Childer-Queen's watching me.

Linna takes my arm and plants a fat kiss on my cheek, and then she swings away like a shoot of hushingstone held in the palm of a dancing Master. In seconds, she's gone—night-swallowed. The half-eaten tongue-fruit is in my hand.

I can still feel the Childer-Queen's eyes on me, like cold drops of rain on my neck. I pull my jacket around me. Her gazing's like a fork in my shoe. I can't walk away, can't move anywhere without hobbling.

Ribbon-tongues cling to black rocks, drift on the water's surface. A crying wind circles me. I hear the Childer-Queen laugh and feel her eyes leave me. I turn to see her at the center of a huddle of Masters. They're tying a red ribbon around her neck as she pretends to protest. Mr. Crowwith is quiet, staring at the Childer-Queen's back as though she's a caged bird that's about to be set loose.

Silence, when you start listening for it, is louder than anything else.

I look out to sea: always lapping and lifting and sinking into calm, always and always and always. I do believe that anything is better than a life behind stone. I do, I do. But I ache for my hollow tree. For the safety of the cloister. I ache, too, for Mother Nine's hurtings. My scabs tingle. At least I knew when they were coming, her lessons of switch and sting.

Don't tell, Delphernia—

I understood the rules inside the cloister.

Out here, the rules don't understand me.

Chapter Eighteen

It's the Childer-Queen's gold-fire gawking that pushes me to do it—to meet Linna at the statue of Rullun Harpermall. It's the Festival of the Sea-Singer, too. I have to get away from picturing all those ribbons as slashed tongues, the sea swirling redder and redder. And Sorrowhall means facing Bly and all the questions he raises in my gut.

But there's another reason, if I'm honest with myself. And it's frightening, the reason, because—

I want to see Linna.

I want to feel as though I am made for my skin again. I want my soul to hum along with a song only Linna's soul sings.

It feels as though the empty streets are getting narrower and narrower, pinching at my elbows. The sky lowers its clouds to catch me in a mist.

I take a seat on Rullun Harpermall's golden boot, resting my head on my folded arms. Rain falls, filling the stone-gouged Featherrut, but I stay still. I don't want to miss Linna.

Finally, I hear footsteps.

Linna is limned in starlight. She's carrying a bunch of tongue-fruit. She looks impressed with herself. Impressed with her loot.

She looks impressed with me, too.

"You came," she says, giving me the tongue-fruit and pulling me up. Her fingers are warm, as though she's touched gold. Her pockets are full of fried and leaf-wrapped seaflowers.

Then her mouth opens like the Childer-Queen's did—opens to the raindrops that glimmer around us, up to the heavens, as if she's worthy of having the sky touch her tongue. As if she's not afraid of it. As if she could swallow lightning. I sway, remembering the tree with keys for leaves, that look the Childer-Queen handed me, my belly so full of unspoken secrets that I couldn't avert my eyes.

Don't tell.

The Featherrut is filling up with rainwater.

"Does it always flood?" I ask.

"Always," says Linna, rolling her eyes. "The water's taken to the Childer for her morning bath—but if you rise early, you can slurp a handful from one of the buckets. It's meant to be good luck."

"Good luck?" Nothing to do with the Childer-Queen seems like good luck.

"It's worked for me so far," Linna says, winking. She looks around, then turns to golden Rullun Harpermall and pushes her finger into his right eye. The statue rises a little off the ground, then slides to the right, revealing a deep black hole.

"What's that?"

Linna laughs at my gaping mouth. "First rule of hiding—camp out under your enemy's nose." She slips into the hole, her feet pattering down a ladder. A few steps and she's gone.

I stare in, my toes at the edge.

It looks like a trap—a place I can't crawl out of on my own. But Linna says my name, and I know I will follow her. Because no one's ever said my name like that. As though it means something terrifying in an ancient language. As though it holds courage in it the way a fruit holds seeds.

"Throw the tongue-fruit down!" she calls.

I do. I hear her catch the cluster in her arms.

"It'll close on its own soon," she says. "It's now or, um, not now." A laugh bubbles up.

I climb down, my shaking fingers gripping gold, my right hand drumming with an almost musical pain.

"Watch out," calls Linna in the kind of shout-whisper that only she can accomplish.

The statue scrapes on its track, clanking over the hole again, and darkness floods in.

I climb down, down, down.

A long way away, a song echoes. I feel like I'm in the shimmer-room again. I started behind stone and here I am — in a place without the sky.

Linna told me she lives in a cloister, but this — the walled-in damp. It's as if I never left. I smell salt and pause, thinking for a moment that the sea has found this place — that it's dripping its cold into the underground tunnel. When I listen closely, though, there's no thrash or spray.

But there is music.

It's a voice. And it's singing a slow, sad song. A song that is a circle, like the cloisterwings' singing. Coming back to the beginning. Over and over and over.

My feet touch the ground. I feel for Linna's arm. "What is this place?" I whisper. "And who is that singing?"

"Singing?" Linna laughs. "That's not singing. It's just the way the wind moves down here—through all the cracks they didn't close up when they built this place. We're alone. I promise."

"How do you know?" I whisper. I feel as though someone's listening to us. Listening to me.

"Because these tunnels—they're a secret the Ninth King never revealed."

"Oh, but he told you about it?" My voice is slick with disbelieving.

"If you must know, my parents purchased the Ninth King's journals at auction after his death. They were artifacts, never touched. Kept behind glass. No one ever read them, out of respect—"

"Wait. You read the Ninth King's journals?"

"Every single one."

The crying voice—what Linna calls the wind— fills my bones. "Weren't you afraid you'd get caught?" I say.

"Of course I was," says Linna, pulling me through the thicket of dark. "But that's never stopped me."

We run. We run.

The singing climbs to a crescendo, then stops.

"See?" says Linna. "It's the wind—that's all. No one ever comes down here."

She leads me to a small room filled with crooked-lit hushingstone. We stand in the doorway, looking in. Potted tongue-fruit trees that have long since died line the walls, their dry, fruitless branches drooping. The pots are made of patterned gold, and the floors and walls and ceilings are stone, just like in the cloister.

"Wait out here," says Linna. "I'll introduce you after they've eaten. They can be a little cranky before they've had their dinner."

They. But Linna said this was a cloister all her own.

Linna hops over hushingstone, rustling dead-bristle branches, the tongue-fruit tucked under one arm. "I'm here!" she calls. "I brought food!"

I hear a shuffling sound and then a squawk—the flapping of wings. Two shadowy shapes launch at Linna, landing on her free arm. She drops the tongue-fruit cluster onto the ground, then takes a fried seaflower out of her bulging pocket and holds her palm flat. The shadows perched on her arm peck at the salted petals.

Birds.

Not just birds, but—

"Cloisterwings!" I say, stepping inside, forgetting Linna said to wait.

The cloisterwings burst into flight. I fall to my knees. I hold out a hand, and one of them twists toward me, flaps its wings to land on my wrist. Linna moves to kneel beside me, tearing the tongue-fruit in half. The cloisterwings seem to prefer the seaflowers, though.

"Hey, save some for me," she says, taking a bite of a crispy petal.

A pang of sadness strikes my heart. And jealousy. They're mine, the cloisterwings. But these birds don't even know me.

Linna points from bird to bird. "This is Mimm," she says, "and Trick."

"Are they girls or boys?"

"Both girls."

"You named them?"

Linna nods.

"Mimm," I say. "Trick."

The cloisterwings stop eating and bend their necks to look at me.

"They know their names," I say.

I never thought to give the cloisterwings names. I knew their eyes. Knew their feathers and cackles. The sounds of their beating hearts as I held them against my cheeks.

"Of course," says Linna. "They're the most intelligent birds ever to exist—at least that's what the First Mother wrote. I'll admit she's likely to have been biased."

"Because she made them," I say, stroking Mimm's back. "But how did these two end up here?" I pick up a seaflower petal and feed it to Trick. "Cloisterwings never leave the cloister."

"The Sea-Singer asked for them," says Linna. "That's what the Ninth King's journals said."

She patters her fingers along the back of Mimm's neck. She looks around the room, then back at me, her eyes wild with secrets. "This place," she says. "The Ninth King called it Hiddenhall. He built it for the Sea-Singer. Because she didn't want to marry him. So he made this secret palace for her, showed it to her one night when the whole city was asleep. And she loved it, loved that it was secret, that she could sing down here without anyone knowing, but there was one other thing she wanted — more than gold and pale silks — and that was a cloisterwing. She told him if he fetched one for her, she would marry him. So he got her two. He asked Mother Nine, and she let them out. But he had to keep them down here so that no one knew."

"Who's been feeding them?"

"I don't know. But they seemed well-fed when I found them." She nods at the trees. "Maybe they've been eating dry tongue-fruit leaves."

"Strange. So you got this story from the journals?"

"It's not a story. It's the truth. He never thought anyone would be disrespectful enough to read his private writings." A laugh claps out of her mouth. "Kings," she says. "Honestly."

I look at Mimm and Trick, their claws clicking on the ground, their feathers glossy as sap. Claws that touched the Sea-Singer's skin. Feathers that knew the feel of her fingertips. These cloisterwings are the closest I have ever been to her — closer, even, than when I brushed my fingertips against her stone-etched curls. I scoot along the ground, edging nearer to them.

"I wonder if they remember the cloister," I say, thinking of the closed-out sky, the damp stone, Mother Nine's hammer-clang steps.

Linna looks at my bandaged hand. "I hope they don't," she says.

I bite my lip, but tears run down my cheeks in itchy streaks.

"Delphernia, I'm sorry. I don't check my tongue before I use it—"

"No," I say. "I was—remembering."

Linna puts her arms around me. I can feel the starry brightness of her hair, wet against my neck.

"A secret for a secret?" I say.

She sits beside me, a smile flashes, and then her face is serious as sea. "A secret for a secret," she says, wiping my tears away with her thumbs.

I look at the cloisterwings. "I sang to them," I say. "When everyone else was asleep." Speaking the words aloud is like loosing a round of hushingstone from my throat.

Linna frowns, pulls back as if she wants to see my face more clearly. "Really?" she asks.

I swallow, heat rushing from the tips of my toes

to the lobes of my ears. But still I open my mouth. "Do you want to hear?" I say.

She nods—one small dip of the chin.

My voice quivers at the base of my throat—a croaking whistle. Linna squeezes closer to me. Her glittering eyes remind me of the First Mother's, and I have to look away. I look at the cloisterwings instead.

Girls with singing throats are swallowed by the sea.

But the sea can't get to me. I am hidden from the sky. All I have here is dark and wings and a girl who says my name like it's a recipe for magic.

I close my eyes.

My voice leaps off my tongue and into the room—a squelchy, spit-shaped note, wavering like a seaflower in a guttering breeze. I let my song lope and roam, upward and downward, not knowing the next step until I get there. This is the only kind of singing I have ever done. It's not as though anyone's ever taught me how to sing songs that have a beginning, a middle, an end.

Mother Nine's voice finds me, says I should have stayed in the hollow tree if I wanted to sing. But I can also hear the Sea-Singer. She's saying, *Don't be silent.*

She's saying, *Sing*. Her cloisterwings are here, after all, like messages from a locked-away past.

I keep singing. I open my eyes and pull strands of light from the air—each note with its own beating heart. I press the light between my palms. Little golden birds spin into being, brushing my ears with their wings. Linna watches them, eyes wide, mouth open. She holds a hand up, and they nuzzle at her palm.

"Mothers of All," says Linna. "How do you do that?"

Mimm and Trick circle my head.

"I don't know," I whisper.

Then the little golden birds gather as one and fly out of the room, searching for the sky, just as they did in the cloister.

"Where are they going?" asks Linna.

"They did the same thing before—flying away. They can press through the tiniest gaps—"

Linna takes my left hand and squeezes. "Look," she says, pointing at Mimm and Trick. "I've never seen them do that before. Flying like that—those slow circles. It's like they're dreaming with their wings."

I swallow, looking up, nodding. "That's exactly, exactly what it's like," I say.

"But the golden birds—they're not shimmer," says Linna. Her eyes are two quizzing moons.

"I can't make shimmer." Another secret, spat onto the ground.

"They haven't asked you to make any? At Sorrowhall? The Prince?"

"The Prince doesn't seem interested in shimmer."

Linna folds her arms. "So he *is* as strange as people say."

I shrug.

I'm about to tell her that she owes me another secret, since I've already told her two, when she throws a palm over my mouth and pulls me to standing, pushes me against the wall. The cloisterwings swoop at my neck, their beaks clicking.

And then I hear it.

Footsteps patter like the beginnings of a stuttering rain.

Linna drops her hand from my lips, and I mouth silent words: "Who's there?"

But Linna only shakes her head. I struggle for air

as though someone's grabbed my throat, as though I can already feel the Childer-Queen's fingers crunching the bones in my wrist. All my hurting places throb. My thumb, my ear, my cheek—

The footsteps come closer, closer, closer—we wait several sap-stretched minutes before they stop. I hear them again, but this time they're getting softer and softer.

Then they're gone.

And then there's silence.

Silence that could strip the sea of salt.

Chapter Nineteen

I'm eating tongue-fruit under the steady watch of stone eyes, sitting on the floor in the room of faces.

The portraits seem to know that I have questions.

But the Sea-Singer's stare reminds me that it takes a questioning girl to do difficult things. And I can still remember the feeling of singing for someone — for Linna, Linna, Linna. Seeing her eyes light up at the sight of golden birds.

My cheeks ache. I realize I'm smiling. Even the dust, drifting like the tiniest stars imaginable, looks beautiful to me.

Until I hear the ringing.

It's so loud, it makes the portraits hum against the walls.

And then Bly appears, leaving wet footprints that tell me he's been at the cave again.

"It's the Bell of Secrets," he says. "They ring it when rulers tell hidden truths."

Hidden truths. Hiddenhall.

Another rumble sounds through stone.

"They ring it a few times in the New Sorrows, then carry it out to the Featherrut—"

But I don't hear the rest of his words. My thumb smarts. I drop the bowl of tongue-fruit. It lands with a crack on the floor. Dust billows, coats my lips. I run out of the room.

"Wait," calls Bly. "Running feet are never wise—"

But I cannot answer and I cannot wait. My eyes would show my guilt. Yesterday, there were footsteps in Hiddenhall, and now the Childer-Queen is going to speak a secret.

I know, I know, I know.

She heard me singing.

Everyone has gathered around the Featherrut to hear the Childer-Queen's announcement.

Wives check their reflections in palmfuls of smoothed gold. Soapstresses follow, some of them holding the hands of small children. Masters laugh, opening their mouths wide enough to take the sun on their tongues. Turnaway girls waft at their sides. Even men who are not Masters have come, their hands calloused, their feet naked. They are the ones who turn shimmer into trays and trinkets, the ones who catch the eels that Mr. Crowwith sends through the skydoor. They are the ones with no musical talent. The ones followed by silence. The ones Blightsenders do not see. The invisibles. I see them. Maybe because my feet were also once cold. Maybe because I know what it is like to see and not be seen.

But I can't think of them now — men and boys who know salt and dirt and metal far better than I. Because the sea is coming for me.

I push past waists and jutting hips, hard backs and soft bellies, to get a clearer view. An old Master spills his drink — tongue-fruit juice, red and sticky — on my shoulder. He says, "Excuse me, miss," before he sees I'm a turnaway girl, his eyes falling on my pierced ear, his face contorting into a look of disgust. "Get out of the way," he grunts. I push on until I can see into the Featherrut through a clash of elbows, staying hidden.

Hiddenhall.

Don't tell.

Mr. Crowwith waits in the middle of the sunken feather shape, a large golden bell at his side. He clangs a hammer against its shining patterns, and the sound rings out again. It's a beautiful sound, but Mr. Crowwith looks as though he's biting down on a knife.

The Childer-Queen appears then, walking past the statue of Rullun Harpermall and stepping down the three stairs that lead into the Featherrut. Her gold shoes tread the ground so quietly that she seems to be floating. The First Mother would be proud. She makes her way toward Mr. Crowwith. The people of Blightsend sigh for her, reaching out to brush her sleeves, which are sewn with iridescent fish scales. Her dress is the color of sea foam. The veil over her face is stiff as a cage.

When she reaches his side, Mr. Crowwith rings the bell again, wincing.

"Today," says the Childer-Queen, "is the Festival of Secrets. This evening, you will send confessions out to sea. But the morning is set aside for my hidden truth."

The Festival of Secrets.

Sounds like a good day for a singing girl to die.

"The Festival of the Sea-Singer always gives me

nightmares," the Childer-Queen continues. "Last night, I crept out of bed without anyone knowing." All the Masters cheer, lifting their hands and clapping. The bells on their sleeves chime viciously. Wives and soapstresses whisper and nod their approval. Turnaway girls are silent. Everyone thinks the secret is over.

But the Childer-Queen keeps talking. "The night had cleared of clouds. I wanted to see the stars."

Whoops and bell-sounds dwindle.

"As I was walking," she says, "I heard a magnificent voice, singing. It seemed to rise from nowhere. From below the ground."

Below the ground.

Hiddenhall.

And still I wait for the Childer-Queen to tell her secret. Still I wait for her to declare my death.

Mr. Crowwith rubs his jaw as though he has a toothache.

"And the strangest thing occurred to me," continues the Childer-Queen. "The voice. It sounded. It sounded like the—"

But the Childer-Queen doesn't get to finish her sentence. Because Mr. Crowwith takes her hand, squeezing her fingers hard enough for her to cry out. She tries to pull away, but he bends to whisper in her ear. He grabs her arm and shoves her away from the Bell of Secrets, up the steps and out of the Featherrut, through the parting crowd and back toward Sorrowhall. She struggles and struggles, but he pushes her on.

Masters clap uncertainly, their sleeves shimmering with bells. Wives fix their skirts, kissing one another's cheeks, as if they're sharing secrets of their own. They clip off on their wooden heels. Soapstresses shuffle. Turnaway girls are led away.

I'm cold inside, like I've swallowed a raw eel. But I'm alive, alive. The sea won't take me today. I trip through the clamor. All I want is to get away from the Featherrut. Away from everything. Away from Blightsend.

But I know that's as stupid as wishing a caged bird into flight.

No one leaves this place—not princes and not Childer-Queens. Not even birds with gloss-sweeping wings. Let alone a questioning girl with nothing but secrets and fear in her pockets.

Chapter Twenty

I follow the coastal road, trying to ignore the careening sky, the smacking sea, until I see Bly on the far end of the beach. He slips into his cave—the one with the sculptures reaching out of its walls. The one with my bird inside it.

My golden bird—its wings beating to the speed of my own heart.

I have to see it. I have to see the bird. It's a mark of guilt, but it's a mark of something else, too. A mark of my voice. A reminder that girls who are broken in their bones can still make something living.

I hate that Bly caged it. But I am grateful, if only in this moment, that he did. Because I can see it again. It hasn't left me like the others.

I run along the beach, barreling into the greedy cave. Caves are gluttons for darkness. Bly has not lit the lamps. There is only the sound of the sea — distant, waiting — and pattering footsteps: Bly's gait, so alive in kept-away places.

When I get past puddles and needle-rocks, I see glimmering wings beaming. The light dances with life, and I know it's a bird — my bird, free of its gustless enclosure. Silently, silently, it's calling to me.

Figures yawn around me, crooking their fingers and swishing their tails. I ignore them. My bird. My bird. But when I am close — so close I can almost touch it — I flinch, pressing back.

Because a groan racks the cave.

It's a searing cry — a scream like someone being born. Like someone dying.

My bird flies away from me until it's only a smudge. I can't leave the light I made behind. I need to feel its warmth brushing my cheek. I force myself to step forward even though my whole body is trembling.

Eyes and hands. Teeth and claws and hooked beaks.

One step, two, three —

A spark glitters. Bly has struck a slice of hushing-stone. He peers at the cave's wall as if it has a face.

"There, there," he says, my golden bird dancing at his shoulder. "The sky is preparing a place for you." He moves to the side slightly, gesturing for the little light-winged thing to come closer.

A giant eye has been carved into the wall of the cave. It clicks in its socket, shifting from left to right.

And then looks straight at me.

And blinks.

Eyes and hands. Teeth and claws and hooked beaks —

The creature — the beast — it can only be a beast — groans again, roaring like a tempest come to shatter the sky.

I turn and I run.

Chapter Twenty-One

There was a groan in that cave. An eye that made it. The groan in the cave. The eye that made it.

An eye can't groan, Delphernia.

Except that it did.

I heard it.

And that sound—that awful, gut-bloomed sound—is still brewing under my skin. It's shuddering through me like the whole ocean is pulling its tides through my bones.

I imagine the eyes Bly carved into the walls of my sleeping-room blinking and twitching.

I picture all his cave-creatures flexing their joints into living. Eyes and hands. Teeth and claws and hooked beaks. I could feel their eyes settling on me. As though they had minds and not just eyes. As though they were alive.

I lie back on my bed, hiding my sight from the walls.

I need some comfort, some hope, so I imagine Mimm and Trick flying at me with force and flutter. I remember them whirling through Hiddenhall when I sang underground for Linna.

And I remember.

The First Mother made the first cloisterwings out of hushingstone.

They came to life between her palms.

What if —

Bly's trying to do the same thing.

I hurry along the dust-clogged central passage of the Old Sorrows, hundreds of tiny windows letting in evening's purple light. I'm leaving a footstep-trail that anyone could easily follow, streaks behind me as if my heels are brushes.

But I have to find the Sea-Singer's library.

Bly was left to his own education there. Maybe stepping among the books will be like stepping inside his head.

"Shhh," I whisper to the thrill of flickermoths in my belly.

But they won't calm their wings, so I start telling them stories.

"Bly says that the Old Sorrows is the same age as the New. After the Sea-Singer was taken by waves, half the palace — the Queen's Wing — was given over to shame and silence. The stone she walked upon was forgotten — banished from memory. That's why it's called the Old Sorrows. It represents the part of Blightsend's Histories that should never be returned to. The part with a singing queen."

The flickermoths flip, twisting up my windpipe. I cough.

"The New Sorrows is the only place the Childer-Queen is allowed to live. When she marries, the one she loves will live there, too. She's never to cross a toe into this place, or risk the sea mistaking her for the Sea-Singer, risen from the dead."

My words echo against stone.

I've reached the end of the passage. Before me stands a door. I approach it slowly, as though it's a new acquaintance. Its gold surface is dulled with grime.

The flickermoths shiver in my stomach.

I open the door and step inside.

The Sea-Singer's library is long and rectangular, a universe of cobwebs, as all other rooms in the Old Sorrows are.

There are no shelves.

Instead, the books are piled in low, haphazard stacks. The stacks are arranged in circles, dotted around the room. Each circle is about knee-high, piled with soft-tangled quilts, as though Bly spends nights here instead of in his bed. The walls of the library—all deepest gray—slope and dip with the shapes of wings and leaves.

I walk around one of the stacked circles, running a finger over gilded covers. The spines glimmer with letters, and, if I listen closely enough, I can hear all the words singing against the pages, as though they're begging for my attention. I kneel on the glimmer-stitched quilts.

"Shhh," I say to the books.

But they won't be quiet.

I pick up a thin volume. It's smooth as wings in

my hands, its cover made out of tongue-fruit leaves. I crack it open, and flickermoths escape from its pages, swirling up to the ceiling. The words are written in octopus ink:

> The turnaway girl is an inevitable contradiction. She makes gold, but she is exiled from it. Perhaps this is because, on the day of her birth, she turned from shimmer as though it were not hers to keep. She knew what she was from the beginning.

I drop the book in my lap. The title glints as I read it: *An Argument for Turnaway Girls*. I roll my eyes, placing it on top of the stack again.

People will use any words they can find to convince themselves that their cruelties are useful. Mother Nine did. And I'm sure Bly has constructed a thousand reasons for keeping my golden bird behind glass—even if I don't have hard enough bones to ask him what they are.

I crawl on my hands and knees to follow lines of leaf-smooth spines, searching for a title that hints at turning stone into beasts.

In the cloister, we read only what Mother Nine parceled out. Our books had pages torn out of them, words turned to ravenous clouds with indigo ink. It didn't bother the othergirls—their eyes only skimmed the world anyway. But to me it always seemed another punishment—tethering my mind to the chopped stumps of her ideas.

Pain seizes my hand.

When I look down, I see that my thumb's turned bloody. The bandage has unraveled, clinging to the sticky, half-healed flesh. I grit my teeth and sit back on my heels, winding it around again.

"I won't find anything here," I whisper.

"You might find the truth," says a voice. "It is the Festival of Secrets, after all."

I look over my shoulder.

It's the Childer-Queen.

She's not supposed to be here. This is the Old Sorrows. I don't think she's supposed to be alone, either. Usually Mr. Crowwith follows her the way a shadow follows a flying bird.

"You left a path in the dust," she says.

I can only swallow.

She keeps on as if I've answered. As if I don't have

a knot in my throat. As if my thumb isn't screaming with hot pain. The books are humming again.

"You're obviously looking for something," she states.

"I was—yes. Something to read." This isn't exactly a lie.

"You know that this was the Sea-Singer's favorite room at Sorrowhall? That's why we call it the Sea-Singer's library, even though it was built long before she was born."

"It was?" I hope she will keep talking. The more she talks, the less I have to admit.

"The Ninth King renamed it. They say he would've done anything for her. They say he was so in love that he made an invisible palace only she could see."

Hiddenhall. Where the Childer-Queen heard me singing.

Don't tell, Delphernia.

The Childer-Queen steps closer. "The thing is," she says, "you and the Sea-Singer—you have something in common." I stand slowly, tucking my hands behind me. The Childer-Queen fidgets with a ring on her finger. Her arm is bruised from Mr. Crowwith's gripping—I can see the marks through the fine silk of her sleeve. "Rebellion," she says, looking straight at me.

I move backward, forgetting the books are there, and trip over them, falling to the ground. The Childer-Queen tramples the toppled pile and stands over me. I could scramble away, sprint out of the library, but I cannot run from what she knows. And she knows everything. She knows how awful I have been—like the Mothers in the whisper-room.

She crouches down to level her eyes with mine. She grabs my arm, pulls me toward her—and hugs me. Her tears wet my neck.

I wait, my body limp, until she sets me free, straightens up again.

She sniffs, wiping her eyes, and looks around the room. "I come here sometimes. To remember her."

I stand. "Girls with singing throats are swallowed by the sea," I say, expecting her to nod and send me on my way.

But she doesn't.

She looks shocked.

"You don't believe that, do you? The *sea*?" She

laughs mirthlessly. "My *father* killed her, Delphernia. With the Custodian's help. They pushed her over the cliff. They *pushed* her into the sea."

I let the words sink, sink, to the bottom of my stomach. All my life, Mother Nine has told me that the sea itself snatched the Sea-Singer from her bed because she dared to lift a quivering song from her throat. And now the Childer-Queen is telling me that she was killed. By the man who built Hiddenhall for her, set cloisterwings to flying for her. The Ninth King—and Mr. Crowwith. Mr. Crowwith, who lurks and spies in his silence, who cannot even stand beside a bell without wanting to clutch at his ears. He hates music. He must have hated the Sea-Singer even more than Mother Nine does.

"Delphernia," the Childer-Queen says, "I want you to sing."

I open my mouth to object, but no sound comes out.

"I want you to sing," she repeats. "In the Garden of All Silences. On the Festival of Queens—tomorrow. I've mourned my mother every day of my life, but we need a *new* singer. Someone to finish what she started." She takes my wrist.

"I can't," I say. "I can't sing."

"But you can. I know you can." Her voice is a pleading threat. "I heard you singing through the wall of the cloister for my brother—I followed him that night. And I followed you to those underground tunnels beneath the Featherrut. I *heard* you."

The sea is calling me, stretching out icy hands to take me. Mr. Crowwith's silence is rushing, rushing like a coming wave.

Don't tell, don't tell, don't tell.

"I can't," I say. "I'm—I'm sorry." I try to move away, but the Childer-Queen grabs my arm like Mr. Crowwith grabbed hers. I blench. We'll have twin bruises now.

"Delphernia, you have to listen to me. When the Sea-Singer sang in the Garden of All Silences, the Masters sang *with* her. The sound of her voice—it shook them out of their stupor. They were moved to tears. They lifted their voices with hers. And they saw what Blightsend really is—a prison."

"That's not what I was taught."

"Me neither. But that's how it happened. If you read the records—" She motions around the library as if to explain where she uncovered this truth. "The thing is, nobody believes it. Even the Masters who were *there* choose to remember the story the Ninth King told with his own tongue before he died. The story the Custodian perpetuated. That the Masters called for her death and the sea obeyed, stealing her from her bed that night."

"They're liars," I say. "They're all liars."

"I need someone to sing in that garden," insists the Childer-Queen. "To remind the Masters of the truth."

But there's a question tickling my throat. "This was only twelve years ago. They don't want change, do they? They like the story they have. They like the power they have."

The Childer-Queen looks at the ground. "They chose to believe the Ninth King's words over their own memories—you're right. But they were scared, Delphernia. They didn't want to admit that the Sea-Singer's song made them see."

"See what?"

"That they were cruel-hearted. That they'd chosen *not* to see. Chosen not to think of how their music kept girls trapped."

"I'm a turnaway girl," I say. "The sea will take me—"

"It's not the *sea* you have to be afraid of, Delphernia!"

But waves are mounting in my ears, and I don't know which is worse: knowing an endless span of salt and gray wants you dead—or knowing the Custodian does.

"You're the Queen—you take the risk." I can't believe I'm talking to the Childer-Queen like this. As though she's one of the othergirls and she's asking me for a bite of stewed eel. I didn't even bow my head and touch my lips when I saw her.

"I wish I could!" blares the Childer-Queen, but then her voice peters out. "I can't sing. My mother didn't give me the gift."

"She didn't?"

The Childer-Queen stares at the ground.

I don't know why *I* got it. This gift, this voice, this curse. I'm only a turnaway girl, and I shouldn't even have questions, let alone a singing voice. I wish I could tear it from my throat and drop it at the Childer's feet. But I can't.

I put a hand to her elbow, gently, and squeeze.

"I'm sorry," I say.

She lifts her fire-gaze. "Then help me."

"No," I say. "I can't."

"Delphernia." The Childer-Queen's eyes are narrowed. "You have the same kind of music as the Sea-Singer. I was only a baby when she died, but I remember her singing. I kept it in my bones—"

I back away. "I am the one who kept music in my bones. In the cloister. And I was whipped speechless for it. You will never understand that."

I start to push past her, but another voice floods the library.

"Childer." The word's a gash in the atmosphere, freezing my feet. "I know you're here."

Mr. Crowwith.

The Childer-Queen wipes her eyes again, tucks a curl behind her ear. She takes hold of my sleeve and pulls me toward him. I yank my arm back, but there's no point in running. Mr. Crowwith has seen me. The Childer-Queen clears her throat, smoothing the spray of her dress.

"Custodian," she says, loudly to mask the teary thickness of her voice. "I know I am not supposed to be in the Old Sorrows, but I smelled sapsweet, and

I found, I found—this girl, Delphernia Undersea. I caught her eating."

Mr. Crowwith's face reddens.

The Childer-Queen tilts her hand, and a sapsweet slips from under her sleeve into her palm, round and golden as a bell. "I found this on her tongue."

I slant my eyes at the Childer-Queen, trying to suss out her purpose. I forgot that eating is a sin on the Festival of Secrets. As far as Blightsend is concerned, girls may as well give up their mouths altogether.

"So you followed her here," says Mr. Crowwith.

"I did."

"And what, as monarch of our great isle, will you decide as her fate?"

"I—I've—" stutters the Childer-Queen. "I've decided not to punish her. The Festival of Secrets is a time of grace. But I have warned her and reminded her that the rules of our festivals run to the very heart of our values as Blightsenders."

Mr. Crowwith is silent for what feels like half a century. I lower my chin, looking at the Childer-Queen out the corner of my eye. Horror fills me as I imagine the punishment I could be in for. No whisper-room this time. Straight to the cliffs.

"Very well," he says eventually. Then snaps his eyes in my direction, being very careful not to meet my gaze. "Remember, Delphernia, on the Festival of Secrets, our lies are enough to keep our bellies full."

I nod. I play along. And I know, I know, I know that I cannot trust the Childer-Queen. Ever. She won't protect me if I sing in the Garden of All Silences. Bly told me: her tongue has hooks. And even if the sea doesn't drag singing girls into its waters, men armed with silence can do their part to ensure that they taste salt.

The Childer-Queen stares at the round sapsweet in her hand. Her tears have dried on her cheeks. "Return to your quarters, Delphernia," she says.

"Yes, Childer," I whisper.

Mr. Crowwith stops me, taking my shirt in his fist. "The Childer might have forgotten that we do not call turnaway girls by their names, but I have not forgotten what you really are. Make sure your shimmer comes to my door tomorrow."

I try to shove him away with the heels of my

palms, but he stands, stiff as stone, before pushing me into the shadow of the passageway.

Right then, I decide. There are more frightening things than monsters made of stone and seas that wait for singing girls to sleep before grabbing at their ankles.

There are monsters made of flesh.

And the Custodian is one of them.

Chapter Twenty-Two

It takes little to make me happy — Linna, one hooked shard of hushingstone, and two black-winged birds.

We're sitting in one of Hiddenhall's underground rooms. Its walls are lined with stone-carved faces, arranged in crooked rows — eyes open, eyes closed, teeth bared, thin-lipped. The expressions change, but the face is the same.

It's the Sea-Singer.

I'll never forget her face as long as I have memory in me. I stared at it every day in the cloister, and sometimes when I close my eyes it's there, clear as I've ever seen it. I see it with my heart.

Mimm and Trick sleep in my lap, their bodies slotted together like two held hands. I stroke their wings, humming songs between sentences.

Linna snuffs the hushingstone, and all the faces disappear. She's wearing her dress of bells again, and every time she moves, she makes music. "How exactly did you live in the cloister for twelve years and not learn how to make shimmer?" she says. There's a lilt to her words that tells me she's at least half teasing.

"Why does it have to be dark?"

"We have to concentrate. Darkness is good for that."

I am more than comfortable being in shadow, but with Linna I want to be in the light. Her collection of smiles is the only hopeful thing in Blightsend. Especially now that she's helping me slither past Mr. Crowwith's threats, teaching me to make shimmer in the blink of a night.

Empty hands must be filled, after all.

Filled with lashes. Filled with blood.

I wonder if Mr. Crowwith has a switch.

"How exactly did you train for twelve years to be a Master and end up with a talent for gold?" I ask in return.

"I believe my question came first."

"A secret for a secret?"

Linna laughs. The sound fills the dark, bright as

any gold. "I didn't learn how to make shimmer," she says. "I mean, no one taught me. I taught myself. The First Mother says if a girl is to be strong, she must be an autodidact."

"A what?"

"An autodidact. Someone who teaches herself."

"But you learned from the First Mother?"

"I read her writings. But I practiced on my own."

I think about the Master who growled at me at the Featherrut when he caught sight of my earring. Turnaway girls are like crumbled bits of hushing-stone to Blightsenders. They're what the city's built on. They're what the city treads upon.

"But why would you want to know a turnaway's trade?" Masters, more than anyone, walk on the backs of cloistered girls.

"I tried to tell you the night we met. The First Mother believed that anyone could make shimmer if they took the time to acquire the skill. She didn't think it was something only for turnaway girls."

Linna can't see me roll my eyes. "And I tried to tell *you*," I say, "that you couldn't be more wrong."

"I'm not wrong."

The cloisterwings stir in my lap. "I am a turnaway girl, Linna. I think I'd know."

"You don't think they teach lies in the cloister?"

I try to match the whisper-room's portrait of the First Mother with Linna's description of her, but it's like writing one half of a sentence in octopus ink and the other in your own blood. Mother Nine taught us that it was the First Mother who said we should be silent—porous for the music of others to flow through us. But then I think of the books in the cloister's library—whole pages scratched to shreds.

Mother Nine taught me wrong.

Everything she taught me was a falsehood.

"All right," I say. "I believe you."

Linna doesn't seem to mind that I took my time coming to this conclusion. "It was my father's fault, probably," she says. "There was a part of me that wanted to be like the magical girls inside the cloister. That wanted to be like any girl, really, because that's who I always knew I was. But my father told me I could never make shimmer. So I had to prove it."

She shifts on the ground, the heels of her stone shoes scraping like a cleared throat.

"I practiced for months. And then, the day before the Festival of Bells, I asked my father to play for me. My father—he's almost as good as me, and he never says no to an audience. Anyway, while he was playing, I made a clump of shimmer the size of my fist. I dropped it at his feet." She makes a sound halfway between a sob and a laugh.

I remember the first time I saw Linna. Even then, her hands were stained with shimmer.

"What did he say?" I ask.

"He insisted that I'd stolen it. Said I'd weaseled it out of my pocket while he wasn't looking. I kept arguing. He refused to believe me. I knew I had to do something. If I didn't—if things stayed the way they were—I would've drowned. So I told my mother. She pulled out her old soapstress dresses. She helped me sew the bells onto one of them, stayed up with me until the sun started rising. And then I said good-bye. I had to say good-bye."

I nestle against Linna.

"What's that for?" she says.

"You don't need to make shimmer to prove who you are, Linna. Even without light, I can see you."

"The thing is," she says, "it's not only about me. I

want all girls to be able to make music — or shimmer, or spotted-eel stew. Whatever they want. And boys, too, I suppose. But that's why I had to leave. I couldn't just be a Master and play music for the rest of my life, and make my father happy. I had to be me. I still see my mother at the festivals — but only for a moment or two. I miss her so much, but I don't want her to get into trouble. I've told her to tell Mr. Crowwith she doesn't know where I am."

"You'll teach others," I proclaim. "You'll do it. I mean, you're already teaching me."

There's a crack in her laugh now. "You owe me a secret," she says.

I hide my face in my hands even though I can't see my fingers in front of me. "I'm broken in my bones," I say. "I've never been able to — Mother Nine says I'm stupid, that I'm too full of questions. That I've decided who I am instead of letting her tell me —" I want to explain everything to Linna, but it all comes clambering out at once in an ever-branching jumble. "There was this baby. I watched Mother Nine make —"

Then there's the sound of something falling. Crashing.

"What was that?" I say.

We choke on our own breath. The cloisterwings flutter against my chest as if my own heart's loose and skittering.

Shuffling, a shout, a muffled scream — then halting, uneven steps.

Click — *click*. Click — *click*.

The cloister rushes back to me — Mother Nine's clanging heels.

"What are we going to do?" I whisper.

"Give me your hand," Linna says. "I've studied the journals. I know this place."

I feel for her fingers. She pulls me, and my feet trample-trip, trying to keep up. I can hear Mimm's and Trick's wings flapping a little way behind us.

My feet skim the ground behind Linna's. There's cold in my bones like a winter wind. And all the while, those click-dragging steps — relentlessly following, following, following.

Then Linna crashes against something unyielding, and I ram into Linna, my cheek stinging against her shoulder blade.

"Where are we?" I whisper.

Linna doesn't answer.

"Linna?"

"It—it ends." Her voice is a claw, a scrape, a cry. "I didn't think—I thought the passage, all the rooms— I thought they were connected. In a loop. That's how he drew it in the journals. It must've been closed off."

She draws a shard of hushingstone from her pocket and ignites it. Fire flares, but I've never been this cold. The wall blocks the entire passage. There's only one way out, and we can't take it—the footsteps are coming from that direction.

"Mothers!" whispers Linna harshly, dropping the stone and stomping on it.

"Shhh," I say.

"There's no point. We're trapped. All we can do is wait."

The darkness seems to deepen.

The footsteps get closer, closer, closer.

Click—*click*. Click—*click*.

And then they stop.

I press against the wall, turning my face away as though I'm about to be slapped. The *shhhh* of struck hushingstone knocks my vision like a punch. And then I see eyes. The Childer-Queen's eyes.

Mr. Crowwith is standing beside her.

Chapter Twenty-Three

I'm pressed against the wall. My throat closes. I can't breathe. I can't breathe—

But Mr. Crowwith isn't looking at me.

He's looking at Linna.

"Master," he pronounces, his mouth crumpling.

I turn to Linna, look back at Mr. Crowwith. I'm trying to keep my eyes off the Childer-Queen's staring, but she's burning my cheek with it. When I finally glance her way, she mouths two words: "I'm sorry." She's leaning against Mr. Crowwith, one heel off the ground. She's injured her ankle.

Mr. Crowwith sneers, still looking at Linna. "There are those who would kill for the honor of being one of Blightsend's finest, Aurelinn Lundd.

And yet you choose to shame the position. That stunt with the dress of bells. Who exactly do you think you are?"

"Call her by her real name," I say, folding my arms. "Her name is Linna."

Mr. Crowwith looks at me as though it's only now occurred to him that I exist. "Very well, then." He turns back to Linna, smiling. "*Linna* Lundd. I'm sure you're both aware that the punishment for hiding a girl-Master is death. And the Childer-Queen *has* been hiding you, hasn't she?"

I step toward him, but Linna grabs my arm. "Don't," she whispers. "It's me he wants."

I glower at Mr. Crowwith, struggling against Linna's grip. "You can't kill the Childer-Queen," I say.

"I can do anything I want!" Mr. Crowwith shrieks. Then he straightens his coat, settles his shoulders. "When the Childer-Queen dies — when the Masters drag her to the cliffs for her treachery, as I have taught them the sea desires — they will turn to me to rule them. And then I, the Custodian of all your noise, will make Blightsend into the place it was always meant to be." He lowers his voice to a whisper. "A silent place. A place without music."

"The sea desires nothing!" I shout. "It was you. You pushed the Sea-Singer into the sea — the sea didn't take her."

Mr. Crowwith only snarls.

"And it would be Bly's throne to take, anyway," I say.

Mr. Crowwith laughs. "That blabbering riddler. Haven't you heard? He's obsessed with the Old Sorrows. Even as a small child, he wouldn't leave the place. Clung to dusty curtains, ignored the helping hand of his Custodian —"

"You trapped him there," I say.

He smiles. "Well, yes. But not the way I tell it. And that's the thing about stories: the teller's more important than the tale."

"If you can do anything you want," Linna interjects, "why do you need me?"

Mr. Crowwith brushes the Childer-Queen's cheek with his knuckles. "The Masters love this pretty little face," he says. The Childer-Queen recoils. "They loved the Ninth King. They even loved the Sea-Singer. I can't simply *tell* of her treachery — I have to show it."

He pushes the Childer-Queen, and she falls forward, her hurt ankle failing her.

"They won't believe you," she whispers. "They won't believe I've been harboring—"

"Oh, but they always do, in the end," says Mr. Crowwith. "It might take a moment, but when they see what you've allowed Lundd here to become." He looks Linna up and down.

Linna scoffs. "I won't go with you. I won't help you lie."

"Of course you will. Because if you don't"—he glances at me—"you must know, surely, what happens to turnaway girls who sing."

I want to run at him, to scratch at his smug throat.

"I know all about you," says Mr. Crowwith, eyeing me. "Silence, more than music, has its uses. The Sea-Singer should've known that."

"Delphernia," Linna whispers, "let me do this." She turns to Mr. Crowwith. "When?" she says.

"No!" I say. "No!"

Mr. Crowwith folds his hands in satisfaction. "Tomorrow evening. On the Festival of Queens. I've told the Masters to meet in the Garden of All Silences. I've told them that they will be pushing traitors into the sea"—he glares at me—"because the waves require it."

Linna's face is white. But she dips her chin. "An oath to the sea," she says.

Mr. Crowwith nods. "An oath to the sky."

A howl lifts in the tunnel. The wind, the wind. The cloisterwings fly along the wall behind us, like the golden birds I made—searching the cloister's dome for a crack to squeeze through.

Linna steps toward Mr. Crowwith. She takes the Childer-Queen's hand and helps her to her feet. The Childer-Queen's eyes are pleading. Pleading for me to do what she asked me to do in the library. But I can't, I can't. They all turn from me—Custodian, Queen, Linna.

"No, Linna—" I say. "Linna! Don't!"

She ignores me. She walks away.

"Linna!" I call. "Linna!"

But she doesn't stop, doesn't turn back.

"Linna, you can't—" I whimper.

"You're free to go now," says Mr. Crowwith over his shoulder. "Your friend has saved your life."

The Childer-Queen's golden heels scuff stone. Click—*click*. Click—*click*.

"I won't," I say, following, grabbing at Linna's elbow. She pulls away, doesn't meet my eyes.

Mr. Crowwith does, though. He looks at me with the force of a thunder-cracked sky. I feel small and scorched as a splint of hushingstone.

"This is a game for kings and Masters," he says. "Not invisible girls."

And he blows out the flame in his hand.

Chapter Twenty-Four

Howling, howling.

It's only the wind, Linna said. But Linna isn't here. It's just me—me and the dark. I've heard my fair share of gap-funneled squalls, and this sound—this is something else.

This is a voice.

But maybe my mind's snipping a story out of nothing.

I whisper for Mimm and Trick, feel around in the empty space, but my fingertips don't find feathers. They find only grit. I narrow my eyes, trying to see around me, but it's like peering through ink.

My heart's a mess of tides. Linna, shimmer, footsteps. Mr. Crowwith. He's taken her. He's taken her. He's going to send her to the cliffs.

The howling voice lifts and lifts. I crouch, crawling tentatively through the blackness toward it. I hold a hand out in front of me until I find the wall that Linna knocked into earlier. Stone stacked on stone. I run my hands along its grooves, pulling myself to standing. No openings—no, there's one, there. I grasp at it, slip two fingertips through it.

I whisper into it. "Shhh, wind," I say.

The sound settles.

And rearranges itself into a song.

It's a looping song, coming back—always and always—to where it started. Like the song I heard when Linna first brought me to Hiddenhall. Like the songs of the cloisterwings. It's coming from behind the wall.

I know, I know.

I hold my ear to the hole, standing achingly still, letting the song curl up inside me.

"I am not the wind," the song says.

Mimm and Trick land on my shoulders, pecking at my ears, telling me to listen. Listen, listen.

The song dips into silence.

"Who are you?" I whisper, speaking into the fissure, smelling damp and salt and seaflowers.

But the singer doesn't answer, only pushes the melody up again, the notes rising like steps.

"Please," I say. "Tell me."

The singing stops.

"My name is Sveglia Emm," says the voice.

"Sveglia Emm." My lips brush against rock. "How long have you been down here?"

"Years, years, years." I hear nails scratching at stone.

I stare into the thickening dark. The cloisterwings shuffle their wings beside me, confusing my ears with feathers. A prick of light catches my eye, and I wait, watching. It's one of my golden birds, pushing its way out through the stone, from Sveglia Emm's side to mine, as though she has sung it.

I turn from the wall and run.

The howling's beginning again.

"The keys," the voice calls, pitching higher. "The keys. The keys. The keys. The keys." Speaking turns to singing turns to screams. "The keys!"

I run all the way to Hiddenhall's entrance. The statue of Rullun Harpermall above me lifts and then slides to the side to reveal the dawning sky, night leached away by streaks of early morning sun.

I hurry up the ladder, gripping the gold-shining bars, my feet slipping.

When I climb out of the tunnel, I look back and see that the cloisterwings have not followed me. They swirl and circle below, far below, the golden bird lighting the edges of their wings as it twists and twirls past them, flying up and over my head. I cannot bear to leave them there. Alone. Without Linna.

"The keys!" I can still hear Sveglia Emm screaming. "The keys! The keys! The keys!"

I whistle and chant, but the cloisterwings won't follow. They must be scared to leave the tunnels, just as I was scared to leave the cloister.

"Please," I beg. "Mimm, Trick." I sing a flutter of notes I made up in the hollow tree, and they settle on the ground, tucking their wings against their bodies and snapping their heads at me. "Come with me," I whisper. My eyes fill with tears.

Rullun Harpermall's statue starts to slide back over the hole. I jump away and fall, my back hitting cobbles. I close my eyes. Tears run down my cheeks.

"Mimm. Trick." I can't go back down there now. Not when there's so little time. Not when Linna is going to the cliffs. My lungs burn. Wings, trapped behind stone.

I open my eyes to the morning's white blearing.

There are two spots in the sky above me. I sit up, laughing, my chest heaving. The cloisterwings. Mimm and Trick—they followed me. They followed my voice.

I didn't lose them. I haven't lost everything. I call to them, and they swoop toward me, clattering their beaks at my ears.

The Festival of Secrets is over. Today is the Festival of Queens. The area around the Featherrut is still empty of people. But it's strewn with little glass bottles with secrets inside them, written on dried tongue-fruit leaves, which the citizens of Blightsend were supposed to send out to sea. Maybe the sea spat them out. Maybe it's tired of secrets. I am tired of secrets.

"A secret for a secret," I croak out.

And then I know, I know, I know.

I know what I have to do.

the
Sea

Chapter Twenty-Five

I run hard through Blightsend's streets, the sun painting stone with a sheen of gold, the cloisterwings'
shadows flanking me. My heart is split down the
center, but it pushes me onward, onward, against a
threatening wail of wind.

To the cave. Bly's cave.

The streets are narrow and empty, bright as needles,
and I can't rinse my thoughts of Linna's face. Linna —
handing herself over. Trading herself for me. And
that voice behind the wall. *Sveglia Emm.* The name
curls its script in my stomach like a prickly vine.

The only thing I can do is beg for help. Tell Bly
about Mr. Crowwith's plan to rid the island of music.
Bly's an odd boy, but he is the Prince of Blightsend.
That must mean something.

I keep running, running along the beach of

hushingstone pebbles, until I get to the screaming mouth in the side of the cliff.

Linna's pale eyes and the strange letters of Sveglia's name push me forward like hurried hands. The cloisterwings fly close at my cheeks.

I can't see Bly. The lamps aren't lit. But I push on until I get to a wall, to the back of the cave, resting my palms against it—then I remember the groan and I push away, stumbling.

But there's no movement. No light. The crashing sea beats against the beach, nearing and nearing, come to grab at my wrist.

Girls with singing throats are swallowed by the sea.

Girls with singing throats are swallowed by the sea.

I'm listening for that sound of hurting. I'm waiting for a monster to burst from stone. I'm scanning the darkness, too, for one little nick of light. But my golden bird is gone. My heart thuds out a mourning, and I clutch at Mimm and Trick, bring them to my chest.

I sit, my legs folded beneath me. A sob escapes my mouth—a small-squeezed sound.

And I remember what it was to let my voice

unfold in an unseen place, with only cloisterwings to listen.

The dark wreathes around me, and I fill my mouth with it. And I am the girl in the hollow tree. The girl who makes birds lambent as stars. The girl who doesn't yet know how hard it is to be free.

My singing is a legion of glowing ribbons. I press each one between my palms until it becomes a beak, an eye, a feather. My tongue is like melted sap in my mouth. Golden birds dry my tears with their wings. The cloisterwings huddle against me, burrowing into my jacket. I'm home. This is the only home I'll ever have: these birds, these songs. The air shimmers with speckles.

And then I hear boots scraping the ground.

I stand. "Bly?" I call.

My gold-whorling birds flutter their light over a face—dark eyes, brown skin.

And then he speaks. "I knew it," says Bly. "I knew you were the one who made them."

Chapter Twenty-Six

The cave billows around me.

I have broken Blightsend's most hallowed law in front of its own prince. With no wall between us. No tulle of shadows. He's seen me. I've seen him.

Faces stare out from the walls. I don't know why Bly spends time here—making eyes and hands, teeth and claws and hooked beaks. I don't know why I thought I could ask him for help. The truth is, I can't trust anyone.

Girls with singing throats are swallowed by the sea.

Waves might not have taken the Sea-Singer, but Mr. Crowwith could still persuade the Masters to push me over a cliff.

A singing turnaway girl.

Mother Nine will be proven right. Mother Nine has always been right.

I get to my feet. Bly takes my hand, but I pull out

of his grip. I turn my back to him, hiding Mimm and Trick. The birds are still huddled inside my jacket, pinching my skin with their beaks.

"Wait," he says. "You made them. I knew you made them." He looks up at the golden birds, his mouth forming words he won't say out loud.

He gives me a chink in time.

And I take it.

I whip around and open my jacket. Mimm and Trick burst out, panicked, flying at Bly with their sky-slicing wings. He jumps back, batting them away in a fury.

I run toward the mouth of the cave, whistling for the cloisterwings to follow me. I trip, grazing one hand on a hulk of rock, soaking my knees in a puddle. I bite my tongue, and that stings, too. I am a pit of pins.

I stagger to my feet. Golden birds fly over my head, swooping like shooting stars as I run out onto the beach.

The tide is coming in.

Water eddies, devouring peaks of rock. Waves lurch and bubble. The cold of the sea frizzles and snaps, splintering the wind, and Bly's footsteps are pattering behind me. Mimm and Trick squawk nervously, a shield of black feathers at my back.

There's nowhere to go, nowhere. The entire beach is swirling with water.

I wade into the thickening swell until I am wearing a necklace of foam. The cloisterwings caw above my head. The tide whips at my ankles, pulls me off my feet into the roiling of the sea. I think of the cloisterwings' soaring and move my arms, but I cannot fly under water. The salt burns my eyes, and I am blind to feathers. I push up to taste the sky. A wave crashes over me. The world tips. I fight against the sea's raging, but it won't stop ripping at my clothes. For a moment, the water takes me in its hands—gently, gently—and I hang, suspended in the gray murk, opening my eyes, closing them, numb with cold. Little fish flicker around me.

The Sea-Singer's voice is in my head. *Sing. Don't be silent. Sing. Don't be silent.* But I can't sing—not here. I am voiceless.

The sea smooths my hair with its fingers. *Finally,* it seems to say.

Remember that and you'll keep your lungs from tasting salt. Mother Nine's words boom in my chest.

I have a singing throat. I have been swallowed by the sea. Girl meets prophecy.

I close my eyes. I close my heart. I close up all the drawers in me, shut away all sound and echo. I sink, sink, pulled down by soaked silk boots and drenched sleeves and bones bursting with music.

But then a rolling surge shoots up, pushing me toward air, lifting me the way the wind lifts a cloister-wing. I gasp at the surface, breathing in deep, hungry breaths, coughing up salt. The water makes a ladder of wave and wind and foam—and then it drops me, pummels me. My knee knocks against a rock, and I grab for it, but my fingers scrape fruitlessly—

And then I'm yanked out of the tunneling froth onto the spine of a bent-necked boulder. It hurts, but it's land, and I'm still, and I'm not sinking. My throat is raw, but my lungs are full of air, air, air, and not salt. Not salt. Not salt. Not salt.

I am alive.

I breathe as though breathing is all I ever want to do. I'm too tired to run, to fight, to fall again.

I open my eyes.

Bly stares down at me, a cloisterwing perched on each of his shoulders.

Chapter Twenty-Seven

Bly has lugged me—limp, salt-soaked, shivering—back into the cave, so deep into its dark that the waves can't reach us. I'm huddled between two sculptures with outstretched hands, hugging his bell-silent cloak around me. Mimm and Trick chirp from a distance, preening their feathers with hard-curved beaks.

I'm cold and damp and the sea's still under my skin—the whole of it, all its sizzle and spray. Rushing, rushing, rushing. I am the whole ocean in one girl.

But Bly's soft voice is calling me. "Tell me how you did it," he says. "If you tell me, I'll keep your secret."

Don't tell, Delphernia. Never tell.

"Please," says Bly.

His eyes are kind.

I can't explain. Not about how I made the birds. It's not the sort of thing you tell about, anyway — it's the sort of thing you do. And, for once in my life, I don't want to sing. I couldn't. My throat pinches. But I want to save Linna. More than anything else, I want to save Linna. And to do that, I need Bly's help. Singing's the only way to get it.

A secret for a secret.

I still the sea in me and fill my lungs with courage. I shiver-breathe, shiver-blink. Everything in me is a clatter of coins.

I picture the Sea-Singer's face — eyes steady in the cloister's carving, in the looming portrait in the Old Sorrows, in the twisted passages of Hiddenhall. She's everywhere. I picture her surrounded by the deathly glister of golden trees in the Garden of All Silences, singing out as though she were alone. That's it — to sing, I need to pretend I am alone.

I close my eyes, imagine that Blightsend is gone.

I open my mouth.

My voice comes out as a thin squeak, pressed against the roof of my mouth, as though it doesn't want to be heard. I push at it, poke it, prod, but it won't move. Won't leave the sanctuary of my chest.

Bly doesn't seem to mind. He sits very still. He listens.

At last, I get a note out—a note that could make something. Full and wing-full. I loop it about, up and down. I smooth its edges against my tongue until it's whole and round—a glow-made globe. But when I open my eyes, there's nothing there—no light-strands. Only Bly's lick of hushingstone flame. Mimm and Trick look at me expectantly.

"It's not working," I say.

"Those who are scared cannot sing," says Bly. "That's from *An Introduction to Voice*, by—"

"Bly," I say, "I don't need you to explain singing to me."

I have to grind my teeth to stop from hitting him in the face. I've only ever sung when scared—and he could never understand that. Neither could the Master who wrote *An Introduction to Voice*.

Bly sits back. "You're right," he says. "I apologize."

He's waiting for a miracle. But I am not a miracle-maker. I'm not a maker of anything. I am a worthless creature. A turnaway girl who cannot make shimmer. Mudworms do not envy me. I have riots in my heart each morning.

I try again. Thank the Mothers, stubbornness is something I do not lack. Bly's words filled me with raging, but he's right. I need to calm my heart to be able to sing, just as I would do in the cloister when I'd settle into the hollow tree's belly and forget Mother Nine existed, become a part of all the noises around me.

I picture the cave rolling like a cloisterwing egg into the waves. I picture it plummeting right down to the sea's bed. I picture me inside it. Right at the center of it, where a new chick would be.

I've visited the sea now. We've become acquainted. I walked into it and it pushed me out. It doesn't want to snake about my ankles, doesn't want to snatch me while I'm sleeping. All it wants is to sit below my skin like a pulse, rush my greedy bones with salt. The Sea-Singer was thrown to the sea by the Custodian. The sea didn't steal her away. And it won't steal me.

I uncoil from time's ticking. And then I sing again. I burrow into the notes.

I am closed inside sound's own palm when Bly shakes me back to livingness.

Light-strands glimmer above my head. I pull them down, press them between my palms. And then there are wings all around us, feathery ovals of lifting luster. They fill the air. They drift as though loosed on the wind. They swoop toward the mouth of the cave and disappear.

I keep singing.

Birds and more birds shudder into living, burnishing the cave with their gold, spinning toward freedom. I run tiny pieces of stone through my fingers, digging while Bly watches the golden birds dip and arc. They brush against his cheeks, tickling his ears, pecking at his hair. He leans forward and lets them perch on his fingers.

Part of me is a banged hinge and part of me is an open window. The fearing's there—of course it's there—but there is something else. A knowing.

Bly has seen the most hidden me.

And he has smiled because of it.

Chapter Twenty-Eight

Silence.

The cave expands like a yawn as the golden birds wing their way toward the sea.

"Thank you," says Bly. "Thank you, thank you." He looks as if he's seen the world's last day and the end is lined with trees.

The cave takes us in its arms. Mimm and Trick settle among sea-beaten scraps of rock.

No one's ever thanked me for singing—no one.

"Delphernia," says Bly, "I need your help."

I remember the groan, the eye, the monster. But now's not the time for fearing.

"And I need yours," I say, meeting his eyes.

"With what?" asks Bly, tilting his head like a bird.

"A secret for a secret," I whisper.

He nods, standing. He dusts his knees and hands.

And then he steps into the dreading dark.

Chapter Twenty-Nine

I follow Bly even deeper into the quiet of the cave. The dark settles around us like sheltering wings. Mimm and Trick flutter at my elbows.

"The golden birds," says Bly. "I caught one when you sang in the cloister—"

"I knew that was you."

He strikes a stick of hushingstone and our eyes meet. "Of course it was," he says.

My breath curdles in my throat.

"It doesn't interest me to turn you in. It never did. I only needed the birds."

"Needed them?"

"It happened by chance. I had almost given up hope, and then—" He runs his thumb along the inside of his cuff. "I've always loved to sit on the rocks and play my stone-flute. The rocks that lead from Blightsend to the cloister's own island. I've always loved to play to the sea. I never believed the waves took her—"

"The Sea-Singer."

He nods. "That night I went closer to the cloister. Closer than I'd ever been. I crossed the bridge of rocks. I played beside the wall. I saw the birds, your eye. And I knew I had to bring you to Sorrowhall."

"Even though I can't—?"

"I don't care if you can't make shimmer."

"You don't? But—" All my life, Mother Nine has taught me that I am broken because I can't make shimmer. Broken in a way that can never be mended.

"I don't," says Bly.

"Why do you need the birds?" I say. "What do you do with them?" I picture the giant eye carved into the cave's wall. My skin crawls with flickermoth feet.

Bly pauses as though he's gathering all the strands of the story in his hands. "The birds you make," he says, "they're not really birds. They're the essence of a bird before it's born in flesh. The part of a bird that doesn't die, ever, even if it's shot down or starves."

I'm sprouting feathers, hearing those words. I'm feeling the wind bristling them. I can make the souls of birds. My own soul flits and glitters like water under the moon. Mimm and Trick nuzzle at my neck.

"The First Mother was a sculptor," says Bly. "She was surrounded by hushingstone, locked in the cloister, so she made companions out of it. Birds. Cloisterwings. They were only dead figures until she sang them souls."

"That's not just a story?" I say.

"It is a story," says Bly. "But some stories are true."

Mimm alights on his outstretched hand, crows as though in approval. Trick nips at my ear.

"The legend goes like this," says Bly. "If a trapped girl sings with trapped birds—birds of feather or birds of stone—and if she loves them, and if the birds love her back, then she'll sing them souls. Souls that can wriggle out of cages, through the tiniest slashes in stone, so that a small part of her—and the birds—can be free."

I think about the cloisterwings in the cloister, gliding in circles when I sang to them, huddling in their nests afterward, sighing in their sleep.

"The First Mother sang souls for the first stone-birds, and they came alive," says Bly. "With beating hearts and warmth under their wings and eggs to lay, living and dying like any other bird. And she kept singing souls for them, even when they were feather instead of stone. So that they could always be free, in some small way. So that she could be free, too."

All that time in the cloister, I was singing souls for trapped birds. And in Hiddenhall I sang souls for Mimm and Trick. Linna said they looked like they were dreaming with their wings, and they were. They were dreaming of flying against an unhampered sky. The golden bird I saw when Sveglia Emm was singing must have been a soul, too.

But—

"There are no trapped birds here in the cave," I say, looking around. "Mimm and Trick have *chosen* to stay with me. They could fly away if they wanted to."

"You weren't singing souls for Mimm and Trick," says Bly.

The eye in the stone. The groan.

I swallow.

"You've been singing," says Bly, "for something I've made."

"Something—"

"Someone."

My skin ripples with cold. I don't know if I want to make a soul for a monster.

Bly turns, shadows sweeping around him. "Come on," he whispers. At first I think he's talking to me, and I follow him, echoing his steps. But then he says, "Come out, come out," and I know he's talking to *it*.

An eye darts in the cave's wall. And then a claw appears, a great wing, a hooked, sharp beak. A monster. A bird. A bird-monster. Its wings are cramped, pinned by stone. It presses out of the wall slowly, crying as it does. It's made out of Blightsend's black, black rock. Hushingstone. Sculpted and sharp-edged, heavy and strong. Unbreakable. Full of fire. The First Mother made the cloisterwings, and Bly has made this.

But it's not only stone.

It's alive.

"Delphernia," says Bly, "meet Uln."

"Uln," I say, stepping a little closer. "That's a strange name."

"It's the name of a poet."

"Oh. I suppose I should've guessed that." I stretch out one finger, draw it back.

"He won't hurt you. He can hardly move. I've

coaxed some of the golden birds—the souls—to drift inside him, but I think he needs more. He's not as small as the First Mother's cloisterwings."

I raise my eyebrows at him. "For someone who loves poetry, you have a habit of stating the obvious." But my heart cracks. This bird has been made in the dark and he is teeming with it. He needs light to fill his eyes. I imagine the cloisterwings coming to life between the First Mother's palms.

"The souls, do they—?"

Bly reads my thought. "The soul of a bird never dies. The First Mother wrote that when her first generation of cloisterwings passed away, she saw their souls leave their bodies and escape through the stone of the cloister. That's when she wrote her only poem."

"Stone bears down in daylight," I recite, "but when nightfall comes, I know that I am flying."

Bly smiles sadly at me. "I love that poem."

"But I don't want stone to bear down on them." My eyes are welling with tears. "They'll be caged within him."

"But he'll be flying, Delphernia. He'll fly across the sea. He'll leave Blightsend. Forever."

"Leave?" I brush my tears away.

Bly takes my hand. "Delphernia," he says, "I need to get away. To fly away on the wings of a bird I made. On Blightsend I only remember the things I can never change: My mother is dead. And my sister is not my sister, even if we share blood. On Blightsend, *I* am caged."

"I understand," I say. I have been caged, too.

"So you'll help me?"

I stare into Uln's glossy eye. A fat tear slides out of it. I move to wipe it away, and he nudges my palm with the crest of his beak. He moans as if he's slipping into sickness.

"I'll sing souls for Uln," I say, keeping my hand against the bird's beak. "But only if you help me save Linna."

Chapter Thirty

"I can't do it," I say.

I collapse on the damp ground inside the cave. Seaflowers grow around me, their petals like salt-sticky fingers. Mimm and Trick jig at my wrists in comfort. I've made about three hundred souls, and Bly has passed them into Uln's great chest, beckoning him out of shadow little by little, but still the creature's eyes are glazed. His wings won't lift with the lightness of flying. And my throat is dry. My bones feel hollow.

Bly paces in the lantern-lit cave. Soon my voice will grow gruff and fade. I'll have to be silent until it comes back. I won't be able to make the golden birds. And we won't be able to save Linna. She's going to die. She's going to die.

"What are we going to do?" I whisper.

With every moment that passes, I am losing her. Losing the girl who gave me hoping. Even Mimm and Trick, snuggling against my neck, can't make me forget.

"Maybe we should rest a bit," says Bly.

It feels more painful to stop than to carry on. But there are only so many souls a girl can sing before she needs a glass of water. Bly tips rainwater he's collected into a wooden cup.

"Here," he says. "This'll soothe your throat."

Mimm and Trick follow us out to the mouth of the cave. We sit, watching the sea move under the sinking sun.

Bly turns to face me. "I've been thinking," he says.

My mouth is full of rain. I swallow. "About?"

"The writings." He scoots closer to me. "See, the First Mother was able to sing souls for the first cloisterwings because she loved them. And I can tell you love Uln—I can tell you love all birds—but I don't know if that's enough."

I couldn't make shimmer in the cloister, and now I can't make souls for Uln. Mother Nine was right.

I'm a wretched, bone-broken girl. I put down my cup. I hide my face in my hands.

"Delphernia, it's not you—it's about purpose. The First Mother made the cloisterwings to be companions. Their purpose was to love her the way she loved them. Because she was lonely. But Uln's purpose—it's not love. It's escape. It's rebellion. It's—fight."

"Fight," I repeat, unsure.

"Do you think—I don't know if it'll work—but do you think you could give your voice claws?"

"Claws."

"You know, make it harder. Make it sound like it has teeth."

I cough and laugh at the same time. "Are you speaking in poems, Bly?"

"I'm serious as sea."

He doesn't sound serious as sea. He sounds like a man who *laps* at the sea and says it quenches his thirst. But I have no other plan.

I drink the last of my water. "I suppose I could try," I say. The cloisterwings chirp, fluffing their feathers on my shoulder. I stroke their backs with one hand.

We walk into the cave again, and I watch the walls, all the creatures Bly has carved, while Mimm and Trick jab at seaflowers.

"Teeth and claws," I whisper, sitting against a carving of an enormous flickermoth. I close my eyes.

And I try one last time.

I open my mouth and I sing.

Because there are some things that make me wish I had claws. Things that fill my heart with fight. They belong to me in the same way the color blue belongs to the sky.

Mother Nine. Her switch. All the bruises she left on my skin. How she tore the nail from my thumb. The babies in their mossy cribs, their sobbing drawn through bone, and Linna, caught in Mr. Crowwith's choke of silence. Sveglia Emm, trapped underground, singing the small escapes of captive birds. And most of all the Sea-Singer, who sang a halo of light in a place that would never grow. One woman, standing in a lifeless place, changing the turn of the tides.

My voice grates out — no longer a flying thing. Tired and rough and tender. Because I'm not singing from the place in me that soars. I'm singing from the place in me that hides in the dark and plots at burning cloisters. The place in me that has a fighting heart, a heart that wants to scratch its way to freedom.

I crawl so deeply into the sound that it takes me away from the cave, takes me back in time. I feel hands grabbing, hear voices rattling. I hear the Sea-Singer. She screamed when they took her children away.

And, in the cave, I scream, too.

My voice echoes: a bleeding, ragged thing.

I only open my eyes because Bly's cold hands are in my hands. I look up and see a rope of light, beaming brighter than any light-strand I've ever seen before. I take it in my hands. It's thick and warm and heavy as stone. There's a thrumming beneath its surface like anger, like will, like a pounding heart.

I knead the light-strand. My ripped thumb bleeds into its burning, brightening its color into richer flame. Then it struggles out of my grip, expanding and expanding. Mimm and Trick bob around it.

"What's happening?" says Bly.

"I don't know. I don't know."

The light stretches, shapes itself, forming the head

of a bird-monster. Dazzling wings fan out above me. The cloisterwings dive into my lap.

A beast hovers above us.

A bird with claws and a sharp-hooked beak, feathers keen as knives.

A bird with fire for blood and blood in her fire.

A bird who's ready to fight.

Chapter Thirty-One

We don't have to tell Uln's soul what to do.

She glides toward him, all fire, flying low under the cave's ceiling. She presses against his stone feathers, looks into his unglimmering eye. She slips into him the way a hand slips into water. Soul and stone merge in a swirl of gold and exploding sky. Uln's eyes remain black—black as mine, black as Bly's—but they're shimmer-filled now. And his feathers are soft, brittle only at the edges.

He's alive.

They are alive.

"He's not Uln anymore," I say, turning to Bly, dizzy with what I've just seen. What I've just done. "Their name. It should be different. They're— they're Nightfall."

"Nightfall."

"From—"

"From the First Mother's poem."

We say the line in unison. "Stone bears down in daylight, but when nightfall comes, I know that I am flying."

Mimm chirrs. Trick flaps her wings.

Nightfall cries out, then surges forward. The tips of their feathers gouge the walls of the cave. They lift their head and look at me, and in their eyes I can see that they know what to do. Find Linna. Be unquiet. Take us away from Blightsend's cliffs. From Mr. Crowwith.

"Nightfall," I say, stroking their smooth-stone beak. They push their head gently against my chest. Their feathers are bristling with life, but the tips are still unbreakable as stone.

"Shhh," says Bly. "Listen."

I prick my ears at the silence, gathering Mimm and Trick into my arms so that they don't make a sound.

A voice echoes through the cave. Not my voice. Not Bly's voice. Not Nightfall's, either. Not a bird or a girl or a boy. A woman. "Delphernia. Delphernia. Delphernia."

Trick tucks herself inside my jacket. Mimm lets out a whimper.

It's a voice like an ax. A voice that still makes me bite the insides of my cheeks. I know it better than I know my own scars. I could never forget it. I'm all welt and wound. My thumb tingles.

It's Mother Nine.

Chapter Thirty-Two

"Delphernia!" calls Mother Nine.

Bly's face is panicked. He smooths Nightfall's black-bright feathers, as though he's already thinking of losing everything. "You have to go outside and talk to her," he says. "We can't have her discovering—"

"You're right," I say. "I'll go."

But my feet have grown into the ground like roots.

I thought I was free of Mother Nine. The law says she's not to leave the cloister—ever. She shouldn't be here. But she is. Her voice is looping about the cave like a hungry spirit, making Nightfall cringe, making Bly sweat. The old scars on my hands darken and sting. *Stay away,* my body says. But Bly settles worried eyes on me.

"All right," I say, "I'm going. I'm going."

Mimm lifts into the air. I ease Trick out of my jacket and hand her to Bly.

And then I turn toward the sea.

Mother Nine stands among the stooped heads of boulder-giants. The sea is varnished with evening light. For the first time since I left the cloister, I feel as though its waters are not a threat. But Mother Nine makes me doubt. Her eyes are on me—reminding me that winter waves have a taste for girls with unruly throats.

I plant my boots on the damp-black beach. I tuck my fingers away and look straight at her face, as if I'm some kind of Sea-Singer.

"You need to listen to me." She reaches out, but I move away.

"You hate me," I say, fight still smoldering in my belly from when I sang Uln a soul. "Why should I listen to someone who hates me?"

Mother Nine knots her fingers. "You need to get out of here," she says. "Sooner or later he's going to find out that you can't make shimmer. If the sea doesn't take you itself, the Custodian will send you to the cliffs."

I let the silence draw her closer to me, and then I whisper: "Bly already knows. I've sung for him, too. Now you can leave me alone. Find someone else to torture."

But she doesn't turn away.

She fiddles with her sleeve, checks the sea at her back as though it's bound to hunt her. I realize all at once that she's the one afraid of waves. Afraid of the world outside the cloister. She taught me to fear it because she fears it herself.

"Come back to the cloister with me," she says. "I'll get us away; that was always my—"

"Always your plan?" My laugh is a handful of scattered hushingstone shards.

I want to spit at her feet, spit out all the lies she ever told me. But I don't. I bury them in the rush and stir of my heart, along with all my questions. I'll turn them to truth with my blood and use them as weapons.

She reaches for my hand again. I snatch it away.

"All I've ever wanted is for you to be safe, Delphernia."

"You don't hurt people you want to keep safe,"

I say, the end of my nose a spark, the corners of my eyes two tiny fires.

"Leave," I whisper harshly. "I don't need you anymore." I clench my eyes closed.

"Delphernia," she says. "If you make this the last time I see you, I need you to know. She is—she was—she was your mother. I need you to know that she loved you."

Her words fill me with the sea's gushing. Mother. My mother.

When I open my eyes, she's put distance between us, weaving among boulders, her silks around her like dirty smoke. She used to seem so big. She used to take up the whole cloister. The whole world. But now she looks small and ragged. Wrinkled and tired, like a dress washed too many times with rough-scrubbing hands.

I run after her—which is exactly what she wants me to do.

But—mother. My mother.

The sea is singing. "Who was she?" I scream, running to keep the mud and feathers of her cloak in sight.

She stops, turns toward me, steps backward, stumbling, her hands two birds. "You won't believe me," she says.

"Tell me," I demand, cheeks wet.

She looks at me, meets my eye for a long time. Then she swallows. "The Sea-Singer," she says. "Her name was Sveglia Emm. I loved her. Like a daughter. She was so gifted. And her voice—I couldn't bear to tell her to be quiet. She was your mother, Delphernia. She gave you that name. Delphernia. It means dolphin—a swimming thing from storybooks."

"But—"

I'm not even sure what I'm going to say. But I want her to stop. To slow down. Mother Nine loved the Sea-Singer. The Sea-Singer loved me. The Sea-Singer gave me my name.

Sveglia Emm.

Sveglia Emm.

The singer trapped in Hiddenhall.

The Sea-Singer is alive. And the Sea-Singer is my mother. My mother is alive, singing the souls of birds deep underground.

But Mother Nine isn't done. She paces back

toward me, grips my arm. "There was a storm after she sang," she cries. "That night. You and Bly were born in it. Twins. And then the sea took her—rose over the cliff and snaked its way through passages of stone to find her sleeping in her bed." She glances out at the waves, quickly, like she doesn't want to meet a stranger's eyes. A stranger she's dreamed of and feared her whole life.

"That's a lie," I say. "The sea didn't take her—Mr. Crowwith did."

Mother Nine ignores me. "After she died, Mr. Crowwith brought you to me. He told me what'd happened. Told me to raise you as a turnaway girl. And he told me to draw out all the new girls' crying. But I couldn't do it—not to you. I knew"—her voice breaks—"I knew she would have wanted me to love you. But I'm afraid I haven't done a very good job of it."

Twins.

Bly.

Mother.

Questions.

Sveglia Emm.

I'm afraid I haven't done a very good job of it.

No, Mother Nine. You haven't.

You haven't. You haven't. You haven't.

Mother Nine grimaces at the sea again. "I beg you, Delphernia, come back to the cloister, and I will make a plan for us to leave this place—like I've always wanted."

"Always wanted?" I say quietly, remembering the whisper-room, the circles she drew around me with her skirts, the missed suppers, my scar-angry palms, my thumbnail torn off and left on stone like an insect's wing, the bruises, the bruises, the bruises.

"You were cruel to me," I say. "I don't understand. If you knew my mother, if you loved her, if you were supposed to love me—"

Mother Nine doesn't utter a word. But she doesn't need to. I know why she was cruel to me. She had loved the Sea-Singer. She'd been gentle with her. And the Sea-Singer had died. She knew that I would have a voice. She knew that I would use it. And she tried to beat it out of me. To keep me safe. Because she saw my mother in me. She saw my mother's crying— my mother's questions—in me.

"You named me Undersea," I say. "Delphernia

Undersea. Because you knew I would go to the waves when you didn't draw the crying out of me."

Mother Nine dips her chin like the good turn-away girl she is.

"I won't go anywhere with you!" I scream, the loudness of my voice surprising even me. I unclasp my earring, pull the gold clear of the flesh, and throw it at her. It drops onto pebbled splits of stone. The sea will claim it.

"I'm a singer now," I tell her, raising my head. "I'm not a turnaway girl anymore. I'm not turning away from anything. And I don't belong to you—I never did. We only belong to those who love us."

I imagine the Sea-Singer holding me in her arms, telling me to sing. I picture us beneath the ground. I picture putting my hand through the gash in that underground wall—squeezing her fingers.

"I belong to her," I say. "I've always belonged to her." I start to walk away, back toward Bly's cave.

"Delphernia—"

"Good evening, Mother Nine," I say.

"But, Delphernia—"

"What?"

She points.

My eyes follow her yellow-nailed finger along the beach's stone, toward the higher ground of the city.

Under a dimming sky, Masters march in solemn lines, no stone-flutes sheathed at their hips. No jeering faces. They're dressed in quiet-embroidered tunics and jackets, unbelled slippers on their feet. No headdresses. They are silent, even if their steps still make rhythms.

My whole body is steeped in cold. My heart grows wings and bangs at my ribs. "They're going to the Festival of Queens," I say. "Linna. I have to go. I have to go now." I tear my eyes from the Masters' procession.

But Mother Nine is gone.

I squint—there she is. Running back toward the cloister. Her sanctuary. Her home.

But it's not my home anymore. The cloister in my heart has burned to cinders, and I'll keep no more wings inside it. I turn back toward the mouth of Bly's cave.

I have a friend to rescue. And a brother to meet.

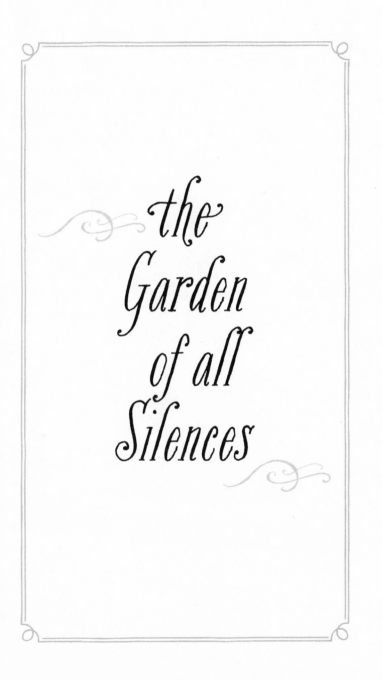

the
Garden
of all
Silences

Chapter Thirty-Three

There are words that knot themselves at your ankles, tie you down with their meanings, and then there are words that light little fires in your kneecaps.

Here's one: *brother*. Bly is my brother.

"Bly!" I yell, running into the cave. Running toward the blood and light we share.

But when I see him, I stop.

He's sitting on Nightfall's back, the cloisterwings balanced on his shoulders. Nightfall arches their neck, lets out a clamoring cry.

"I went looking for you," he says. "I saw them — the Masters. We don't have much time." Nightfall lurches underneath him, almost flinging him off their back. "They want to fly," says Bly, clinging to the beast-bird's feathers.

I can see that.

Even if the whole sky was torn to pieces, this giant bird would fly, up and up and up, finding new skies, new stars to press their wings against.

Bly says, "You'll have to jump."

"What do you mean?" I laugh out the words.

Before Bly can answer, Nightfall glides forward as if they're made of howling wind, lifting into the air and grinding their head against the high ceiling of the cave. Bly says, "Now!"

Nightfall's wings spread out like seeping ink, clicking like warming bones. In their glistening eye I can see the soul I sang. The cloisterwings cry out.

Bly says, "Come on, Delphernia! Jump!"

My brother. Bly. My brother says jump.

So I do.

Chapter Thirty-Four

I leap, reaching out, limbs and flame and brightness and fear, jumping—*flying*—forward.

I land on Nightfall's back, legs dangling, a searing pain in my right thumb. Mimm tugs at my jacket with her beak, and Trick circles my head.

Nightfall picks up speed, sweeping out of the cave's mouth into the gentle light of evening.

Bly pulls me up, my thigh grating against the grit-crumbling edge of an armor-like feather. And then I'm seated on the back of a monster-bird.

The wind whips loosened curls across my eyes, and my mouth is full of salt and sky. The cloister-wings are soaring, soaring, as though they've never been trapped.

And I don't care that I'm scratched and bleeding—I'm flying.

We are flying.

Together.

Chapter Thirty-Five

The wind blows hungrily. I can't get away from it, no matter how high Nightfall lifts in the air. Mimm and Trick fly above us, giving Bly a headdress of feathers. Bare-risen stars wink like eyes.

We soar over hunched boulders, over the silver edge of a winding cliff, veering left toward the dead-gold garden.

We hover over it, looking through the slivers of space between moonlit branches.

The Childer-Queen sits on a throne that's been cobbled out of wood and shattered glass. A harsh-cut hushingstone crown is balanced on her head. She is sobbing. Mr. Crowwith stands calmly at her side, his hand grasping Linna's arm.

Linna.

She's still wearing her dress of bells.

We wait as the Garden of All Silences fills with hundreds of Masters.

They stand in a circle around the Childer-Queen, Linna, and Mr. Crowwith. A barricade of unspoken threats.

My heart feels as hollow as a half-burned tree. Nightfall tilts in the air. I grip their feathers. Their flying depends on the fight in my heart, just as the first cloisterwings' flying depended on the First Mother's love. I remind myself that if my voice can make the souls of birds, it can do anything, and Nightfall steadies, teetering in the battered air.

The wind quiets down, wrapping me in its silken cold, and with my heart I tell Nightfall to lower to the ground.

Nightfall's claws meet lungmossy stone. They spread their wings to crack at golden bushes, snapping trees that judder and fall. Even the tree with keys for leaves is thrown to the ground with a creak and crash. Masters scatter, covering their heads, unable to cry out without breaking the laws of Blightsend. They stare at us as though Nightfall has come to lead them to the door of death.

Mr. Crowwith's face warps with confusion. Dread.

I stand up on Nightfall's back.

I fill my lungs.

I find my voice.

And, in this silent and dead place, I speak. "Give Linna and the Childer-Queen to us and we will leave peacefully."

As if in agreement, Nightfall screeches. The sky buckles. The Masters narrow their eyes, mouths opening without words. They are watching me. But Mr. Crowwith is watching *them*. He knows they will do what they've been told the sea requires.

He clears his throat, and they look back at him. He motions for them to approach the traitors. They seem to forget about me. About Nightfall. They form a ring around Linna and the Childer-Queen again.

I freeze.

Nightfall freezes, too.

I sit down, then slide off Nightfall's high back.

"Delphernia—no—" whispers Bly, the cloister-wings flapping their wings frantically at his cheeks.

"I have to do something," I say.

The Masters' eyes pelt me, their faces torn into

scowls, until they see the cloisterwings flying at my side. They touch fingers to lips and bow their heads, eyes wide and searching.

Then they turn from me, tightening around Linna, Mr. Crowwith, and the Childer-Queen, closer, closer, closer — silent as shadows.

I remember what the Childer-Queen asked of me in the Sea-Singer's library. To be the girl, singing in the garden, who changes everything.

Sing. Don't be silent.

Mimm and Trick spin at my throat.

I gloss my tongue with spit. I ignore the tremor in my bones, the thump in my chest. The sea raises its head to listen. I breathe. I breathe. I breathe.

And then I push a rising note out of my mouth.

Chapter Thirty-Six

The note thickens the air like mist.

I draw it out, letting it bloom and loop and quiver.

Mimm dives and twists. Trick caws.

No light-strands shimmer in the air above me, no golden birds spread glisten-spark wings, no souls erupt against deepening heaven.

I am not trapped. I am singing freely.

The Masters part, turning their heads to me as though I'm speaking a language they haven't heard since they were small enough to fit in cribs. The ones holding on to Linna let go of her jingling sleeves. The others' hands drop to their sides. They listen. They are listening to me.

I keep my eyes open. I want to see it when it begins. Want to see their faces change as their ears fill with something they've only ever heard once before—if they've heard it at all. A girl singing. A girl singing in the Garden of All Silences.

And not just any girl. The Sea-Singer's daughter.

"You sound like her," says an older Master, breaking the law with his tongue.

Some of the others nod, whispering among themselves.

The Childer-Queen smiles, her cheeks traced with tears.

I look out over the sea, wrenching my most hidden voice from my belly. Then the sky softens the edges of its clouds, sets to falling a dusted rain, and I stop singing. I stretch out my tongue. I swallow the sky.

Mr. Crowwith is staring at me as though I'm a ghost—the long-buried come to kiss his cheek. His attention scatters, and Linna sees. She jams her stone heel into the toe of his silk-and-gold boot, her elbow into his stomach. He clutches at his gut, and she runs, pushing past distracted Masters. She runs to me. She takes my unhurting hand.

"Keep singing," she says, as all the Masters turn oily eyes on us.

I lift my voice again.

Linna stands behind me, letting the music drift through her bones. At her back, light-strands form. She turns to draw the glowing notes from the air. By the time I let my song sink into silence, there's a knot of lustrous gold resting in her palm.

She tosses it into the crowd of Masters. One of them catches it. The others gasp. They hover fingertips over the shining metal.

Mr. Crowwith tries to push through the crowd, but the Masters have formed a wall of elbows, leaning in to get a closer look at Linna's shimmer.

The sea spreads its waves into silence. The Masters move slowly around us, holding up their hands to show they mean no harm. Their whispers ripple like lapping waves. Their eyes are like darting fish.

Then a shriek rumbles the ground beneath our feet. "Wretched gold-lickers!" It's Mr. Crowwith. "You give wings to traitors with wicked tongues. You ignore Histories on the whim of a pretty voice!"

The Masters turn toward him, opening a path in their midst.

He bolts through the narrow gap, grabs and yanks

Linna's wrist. He motions to the Childer-Queen's cobbled-wood throne and a group of Masters takes hold of it. Her face is crumpled in fear. They start dragging it toward the cliffs. Mr. Crowwith pulls Linna away from me, struggling through the crowd of Masters. The Childer-Queen screams.

The wind takes a cue from chaos. It starts ripping at my ears again. Shouts and whispers. Hair stinging at my cheeks. Bly's whistle. When I snap my head back, I see Nightfall lifting into the air. Mimm and Trick have flown to sit beside Bly on the great bird's stone back.

I have to get to Linna.

I have to get to Linna.

I run toward the cliffs, pressing past sleeves, biting and clawing to make my way through. I can see Linna's shining hair, the Childer-Queen's crooked stone crown.

"Wait!" I scream. "No! Wait!"

Then I can't see Linna—or the Childer-Queen.

And the Masters have stopped walking forward.

I tear past them.

Mr. Crowwith is standing at the edge of the

cliff beside the traitor's throne he fashioned for the Childer-Queen. But the throne is empty. He is alone.

"Linna!" I stagger, skid.

And see her.

She's falling through the air, a grain of gold, luminous against the unforgiving gray of the ocean. And the Childer-Queen is the sparkling wing of a flicker-moth, thrown into whipped cloud.

Chapter Thirty-Seven

Something scrapes at my shoulder.

I howl, turning my head to see an immense wing blocking out cloud — stone-dark and knife-sharp.

Bly grabs my hand. Mimm and Trick hit my chest, scrambling underneath my jacket. I'm swept onto Nightfall's back.

Nightfall pushes on, into the bellow of the wind. I grip their salt-crusted feathers with bleeding hands, tears streaming down my cheeks.

We keep steady, flying down, down, down, and all I'm hoping is that we'll be able to do it — to catch Linna and the Childer-Queen on Nightfall's broad back.

But then I see the cloister.

The cloister, distant, its own island.

Burning, burning, burning.

A blister of flames against the sea's surface.

The bridge of spike-sticking rocks between the

cloister and Blightsend's farthest border is peppered with tiny figures—loosed turnaway girls. They're free. But the cloisterwings. All those cloisterwings—

Mother Nine would never think to let them out. They're trapped in there. I know I'm too far away for it to be real, but I can smell charred feathers, can hear songs choked by smoke. I can even taste the metallic tang of melting shimmer. Mimm and Trick tremble against my chest, and I am filled with a harsh, piercing silence.

My heart loses all its fight.

And when my heart's not fighting anymore—when it empties of storm and sound—Nightfall cannot live. Their golden soul slips out of their body. For a moment I can see the soul I sang—the monstrous soul that came from my bones—against the wide blackness of the sky. But then she soars off. Another gold-feathered bird lost forever. Nightfall's wings—*Uln's* wings—shatter like hammered glass beneath us.

And I am falling.

We are all falling.

Chapter Thirty-Eight

All I hear is the sea, the sea — reaching up to take me.

My skin is covered in fine dust — in the remnants of Uln's wings. Mimm and Trick burst out of my jacket and clobber my ears.

They're coming for me — waves with sharp teeth of crystallized salt. My body whips through space, all ache. I close my eyes.

Girls with singing throats are swallowed by the sea.

Mother Nine was right.

Here it is, swelling like a bruise —

And I feel —

Feathers.

Feathers. Not water. Not ice-shard waves. I feel the

pinch of beaks. I'm not falling anymore. Not falling—but not rising, either. My heart skips, uneven, and I hang above the crashing sea, the sad songs of birds surrounding me like a garden unfurling.

When I open my eyes, I see the night sky. Mimm and Trick squawk over me. Theirs aren't the feathers against my neck and behind my head. Brushing my wrists, my ankles, with their edges. Feathers underneath me.

It's the cloisterwings.

Mother Nine set them free before she lit their home on fire.

And they came for me.

They're lifting me up, slowly, slowly. Beaks pull at my hair and wings pump against the wildness of the wind. They've made a net of black feather and wing-shine beneath me. They are lifting me on their backs. But it feels as though I am held only by the sweet tones of their voices.

I watch Uln's remains—gray as ash—shift like a thundercloud, landing on the surface of the sea like a fall of distant rain. I drift upward, upward, upward, through layers of mist. Chills ruffle under my skin.

There are other groups of cloisterwings on

either side of me, lifting the others on their backs, too, some of them fluttering between us. Bly clasps my hand. Linna's caught up, too, lying still on a bed of black feathers, her mouth open in shock. The Childer-Queen's delicate silks are tugged through gathered cloud by the gripping claws and clicking beaks of the First Mother's birds, wings beneath her and wings above her.

Wings beneath all of us, as though the wind has learned of singing.

Chapter Thirty-Nine

The cloisterwings lower us into the Garden of All Silences, among broken branches and gold-crushed petals. They form a whirling wall to keep the Masters away from us, snapping beaks and flapping wings in a scratch-scattering flurry. Masters gather silently, the birds scrabbling at their cheeks if they come too close.

"They saved us," says Bly. "You sang souls for them. You helped them escape the cloister long before Mother Nine opened the skydoor—and they saved us."

Even though I'm lying on the ground, my bones still feel like they're falling. My stomach is inside out. My ears are stuffed with silk. "Linna," I choke. "Where's Linna?"

"I'm here!" She collapses on top of me, laughing,

then rolls over onto her back, the music of her dress shimmering. "We were flying!" she says, as though she can't believe it.

I laugh, wincing as my ribs ache. Leave it to Linna to think of falling as flying. Tears stream silently down my cheeks. I sit up slowly, pressing my palms to the lungmossy ground. It's solid, unmoving. I'm not falling anymore. I'm not falling.

Then the Childer-Queen is standing over us, her arms folded. Bly gets to his feet, dips his chin. Linna blinks up at the Childer-Queen's face—irreverent as ever.

"Childer—" I say.

But when I look up, she's holding out a hand. "We've never been properly introduced," she says. She looks at me, then at Bly, then lets her eyes rest on Linna. "None of us has. My name is Fable—Fable Harpermall. Thank you for—"

Her words are cut off by Mr. Crowwith's low voice. He's elbowing his way through the crowd of Masters, scowling at their shocked faces. "Your cloister is burning!" he screams at them. "Your cloister-wings are loosed. And a girl—a *turnaway girl*—has sung in your garden. A child born in music has made shimmer." His voice gets louder with every word. "Will you not stand up and be Masters? Will you not choose for yourselves a ruler to replace your treacherous Childer-Queen?"

The wind bays. The cloisterwings break the light around us with their wings. In glint-glimpses, I can see the Masters squinting at Mr. Crowwith's reddened face, at the fire and billow of the cloister.

Bly squeezes my hand. The Childer-Queen sits down beside Linna, who gets to her knees and puts one arm around me.

One of the Masters speaks. "The Custodian is right," he says. "And I can see only one who would rule me."

Mr. Crowwith purses his mouth and straightens his shoulders, readying to hear his own name.

But the Master turns away from him.

He peers into the brokenness of the Garden of All Silences—the fallen trees and crooked branches, the split leaves and smashed buds. He dips his chin, closes his eyes, touches fingers to lips. And then he kneels—to the tree with keys for leaves. It's lying on its side like a toppled giant, uprooted by Nightfall's wings.

The moon is ablaze in the sky, and its light is banging off angles of gleaming gold, and there—through the frenzy of wings—I can see her. Standing tall, her skin a glowing brown, her hair a dark-crimped diadem. She's wearing bracelets of golden cloisterwing souls.

One by one, the Masters turn their heads. They kneel.

"Is that—?" says Linna.

Mr. Crowwith's face is blanched.

It's the Sea-Singer.

Chapter Forty

The Sea-Singer steps tentatively toward us, as though she's teaching her toes what it feels like to walk on lungmoss again.

She holds her hand up to the wall of cloisterwings, and they lower in one swift motion, rushing at her skin like a winged gust of wind. Mimm and Trick snuggle against my neck before alighting on her shoulders.

"You're not caged anymore," she says, as though she is talking not only to the birds but to herself.

The cloisterwings soar, one cloud of wings, flying up and flying out, over the sea and into the light of a thousand stars. The golden souls tipping the Sea-Singer's fingers follow.

Mimm and Trick hang back, clinging to the worn silk of the Sea-Singer's dress. They caw mournfully, blinking their eyes against her cheeks. Then they swoop after the others.

I watch them go.

The Sea-Singer crouches before us—before me and Bly and Linna and Fable—spreading her arms to take us all in.

Warmth. Skin against my skin. Hair smelling of dust and blood.

When she pulls away, she holds her palms to my temples. "I knew it was you," she says. "Delphernia Sveglia Harpermall."

The Sea-Singer—my mother, my mother—stands, turning toward the kneeling Masters. She looks over the tops of their heads. Looks at Mr. Crowwith.

"Bind his hands," she says.

"Sveglia—" he cries. "You must understand—I only did what the Ninth King asked of me—" He struggles against the Masters encircling him.

"And now the Masters will do what *I* ask of *them*," says the Sea-Singer, turning to face us again, ignoring Mr. Crowwith.

"Sveglia!" he screams.

She snaps her chin in his direction. "Why don't you show off that silence you're so famed for," she says sweetly, "and close your mouth."

Chapter Forty-One

In glistening night, I walk through what was once the Garden of All Silences. It's filled with the smell of soil and the promise of new leaves.

One day, there will be a tongue-fruit tree for every soul who loved me enough to listen to my voice. One for Linna. One for Bly. One for Fable. One for each of the cloisterwings. And of course there'll be a tree for the Sea-Singer.

My mother.

Our mother.

Voices lift from a distance, darned with the strains of stone-flutes. Tonight is the Festival of Shimmer. The Masters have collected the gold that Mr. Crowwith makes in his underground prison. They're weighing it now on the beach, eating sapsweet puddings as

Linna teaches them how to knead the fresh glow of music into metal—and how to improve their playing. She's an education for their ears.

I look across the sheen of the ocean, following the path of rocks to where the cloister used to be. It's only a pile of burnt hushingstone now. Mother Nine has a grave there. I do not visit. Sometimes her words still kick up in my heart, but I've learned to dampen them with singing.

We found the loosed turnaway girls crouched among boulders, shivering, the older ones holding the babies. They live at Sorrowhall now. The ones my age and younger still don't have questions, but they like to shine polished gold, catch warped glimpses of their eyes in sun-skimmed plates. Some of the older ones have made themselves little crowns. This pleases Fable.

I open my mouth and a song unwinds from my chest, but there's no gleam pushing through.

I haven't sung the souls of birds since the day I met my mother. To make a bird's soul, the singer must be trapped, and I'm done with that—I'm free.

And so are the cloisterwings.

Sometimes I feel Mimm and Trick nudging my cheeks as I'm waking from sleep. Then I remember they're gone.

But I am not afraid.

I won't worry for feathers.

I've planted a garden, and I know—I know, I know—the birds will come.

Acknowledgments

I could not have written this book without my brilliant agent, Patricia Nelson, who pointed the way to Blightsend. Thank you for believing in my work from the very beginning, Patricia. You have made my biggest dreams come true. Here's to many more stories about magical girls with secrets.

Miriam Newman, my phenomenal editor, helped me turn an unruly manuscript into a book. Thank you so much, Miriam. Working with you has been a gift. I couldn't have done this without your insight, passion, and determination. Thank you for loving Delphernia and Linna as much as I do.

To everyone at Candlewick Press and Walker Books: thank you for working so hard to get my strange little book out into the world. Special thanks must go to Pam Consolazio for making *The Turnaway Girls* prettier than I ever could have imagined, and to Sarah J. Coleman for creating such an evocative jacket for this story. (Sarah, you sing with ink!) Thank you to Betsy Uhrig and Hannah Mahoney, both brilliant copyeditors, for noticing the details, and to Maggie Duffy, Emily Quill, and Martha Dwyer for catching inconsistencies. And a big, big thank-you to Karen Lotz for reading and suggesting changes.

To every person who read a version of *The Turnaway Girls* and offered advice: thank you. Your input has helped me shape this story into something I am proud of. I especially want to thank Susan Bishop Crispell, Kathryn Rose, and Heather Clark for their words of wisdom and encouragement. And thanks to Kheryn Callender for reading the earliest version of this story and cheering me on.

To my teachers: Mrs. Knight, who helped me believe I was intelligent enough to write in the first place, and Mrs. Krall, whose kindness got me through high school. Thanks to Alison Lowry, my first creative writing teacher, who told me not to be afraid of dark endings, and to the professors at the University of the Witwatersrand who deepened my love of languages and literature: Claudia Gianoglio, Alida Poeti, Tim Trengrove-Jones, Gerald Gaylard, and Merle Williams. *Grazie mille.*

To Kate Paterson, who, when I told her I was writing a novel, said, "Of course you are!" Kate, meeting you made five years of legal education worth it. Thank you for not doubting.

To my *ouma*, Petrusa Johanna Spies, who taught me to watch for fairies in the garden. Your imagination has inspired mine. Thank you.

To my sisters, Tamsyn, Chelsey, and Ashley Chewins, whose soul-shapes match mine. Thank you for teaching me what friendship is.

To my niece, Tatum Seymore, who said, "I want to read that!"

To my parents, Mark and Linell Chewins. Thank you for supporting me on this path. Thank you for loving me so much I couldn't help but think I was capable of anything. You are my definition of extraordinary.

To my husband, Liale Francis, who looks after me in every possible sense and who introduced me to the songs that inspired this book. Liale, you are the best thing that's ever happened to me. It would take a thousand pages to detail all the wonder you have added to my life. So I will just say this: thank you for everything. I love you.

Last, to Darfer, who reminded me who I was when I had forgotten.